THE P

THE PUDDLE PEOPLE

3 Spot Press

Tommy Ellis

For Steve - A great drummer, and a true cat person

"We don't do these things because they are easy, we do them because they are right." - Lake Splashdown.

CHAPTER 1

Bank Holiday Blues

Sunlight glinted off the brass cogs and clock gears of the home-made model car. It bounced along the garden path, electric motor whining in the warm still air. At seven in the morning it was already sweltering. The late summer heatwave had lasted for nearly four weeks, making it one of the hottest on record.

'Ethan, come in now. We'll be going soon.' Mum's voice drifted from the kitchen, along with the sizzle of frying bacon. The delicious odour of a full fried breakfast wafted from the house. It was the smell of holidays, and this was going to be a good one. He'd been looking forward to the week away at Golden Sands Holiday Village for ages. The crazy golf tournament was top of his activities list. He'd been practising all year with ping-pong balls, a coffee cup and Dad's five iron.

Eleven-year-old Ethan Myles was about average height for his age. He had a mop of uncontrollable spiky blond hair and wide-set blue eyes. With a pair of oversized feet he hadn't quite grown into, he could easily be mistaken for a garden troll.

'Coming, Mum.' He bent down to scoop up the quirky looking car, when a flash of black and white shot out of the flower beds almost tripping him over. 'Jimmy, you maniac!' The cat leapt onto the fence and regarded Ethan coolly from the top of the shed. Ignoring the cat's steady gaze, Ethan reached down once more to retrieve the car. That's when he spotted something glinting from amongst the roses. The dappled sunshine that filtered through the oak leaves reflected a sparkling light. Frowning, he stepped off the path and knelt to take a closer look. The cat had unearthed a pale pink crystal that now lay on the surface of the flower bed. It was about ten centimetres long and shot through with flecks of gold. Ethan picked it up and stared at it, squinting slightly. It was quite beautiful. Fixing his gaze on the glittering sparks of gold, he thought he could see some of them getting bigger and then smaller again. All of a sudden it pulsed, warming his hand at the same time. Ethan let out a bark of surprise, almost dropping his new artefact. He shook his head and rose to his feet, hastily making his way to the breakfast table, when a curious humming came from the quartz. Deciding his imagination must be working overtime, he slipped the crystal into his jeans and stepped through the kitchen door.

'How many times have I got to tell you not to wear your slippers in the garden? Where are your trainers?' Mum shielded her mouth with her hand and coughed. A low bubbling gurgled from deep inside her lungs.

His parents tried to play it down, but Ethan knew his mum's health was a lot worse than they let on. The tablets had worked for a while, slowing the disease. They had even reversed the symptoms for a time, but when the portable oxygen tank came home on its trolley with a squeaky wheel, Ethan knew the drugs had stopped working.

'I dunno.' He rummaged around in the kitchen, tripping on the cat's food bowl, sending a shower of biscuits across the floor.

'Oh, for crying out loud!' Mum heaved in a rattling breath. 'I'm trying to make breakfast.' She stopped to take another breath, the faint hiss of oxygen barely audible above the crackle of bacon. 'And if you don't watch out, you'll be wearing it instead of eating it. Get out from under my feet and go and check in your bedroom.'

Ethan's bedroom could be likened to a mad professor's laboratory. Half-finished electronics projects littered the desk under the window. A large white robotic arm with wires and circuit boards spilling from its insides lay sprawled across the unmade bed. 'Mum,' he yelled from the top of the stairs. 'They're not in my...' They appeared, dangling in front of his face, like magic.

'You left them in my room when you borrowed my phone, you numpty.' Waving the smelly foot-wear under his nose, Ethan's nine-year-old sister, Amber, brushed a stray lock of otherwise per-fect blonde hair out of her face. 'I found them by following the smell. You really are disgusting.' Wrinkling her nose, she held the Reeboks by the laces. 'Take them before I puke, you rancid pus bag.' Gagging, she ran back into her room.

'Pus bag yourself!' he yelled at the closed door. Ethan sniffed his top-of-the-range running shoes. She had a point, though. The stench that wafted from the depths of his boat-sized shoes could have floored a sewerage worker.

'Come on, eat your breakfast and get in the car!' Dad's voice boomed from the bottom of the stairs. 'We've got to get going.'

They were driving along Chestnut lane in bright sunshine when the heatwave broke. Daylight gave way to heavy grey clouds, and sheets of rain pelted them from all sides. Wind buffeted the old Ford as the windscreen wipers flapped uselessly against the deluge. White jags of lightning forked across the darkening sky, followed by a deafening clap of thunder.

'That was close.' Dad glanced nervously at the sky. A second lightning bolt sizzled overhead followed by a loud bang.

'Dad, look out!' screamed Amber.

A huge bough ripped from the old oak tree on the village green and crashed across the road.

'Hold on tight, everyone!' yelled Dad, as he jerked the steering wheel to the left and accelerated hard. The car slid sideways and with a squeal of tyres, went into a spin.

Ethan gripped the back of Dad's seat and squeezed his eyes tightly shut, bracing himself for the impact. The car screeched left, then swung right, before glancing off the fallen branch with the sound of grinding metal. The air filled with oily smoke as the car's engine screamed and then died with a clattering bang. Ethan opened his eyes. Dad leaned over the back of his seat.

'Are you kids OK?'

Thick blue smoke poured from under the bonnet.

'Dad!' yelled Amber, 'the car's on fire.'

Dad sighed. 'No, we're fine. The throttle must have jammed, or something.' He shook his head. 'The engine's blown.'

'What about the holiday?' asked Ethan.

'There goes the holiday.' Dad pointed through the windscreen at the thinning plumes. 'Up in smoke.'

'Come on, everyone. Coats on and hoods up,' said Mum. 'Last one home puts the kettle on.'

The storm had caused the worst power cut they

had ever known. Not only was there no electricity, but to Ethan's utter dismay, no electronic signal, either. This meant no computers or cell phones. It was like living in the dark ages, with just the open fire for heat.

'This is just perfect,' said Ethan. 'I would have won the crazy golf competition for sure, this year.'

'Yeah, well. If you hadn't left your revolting trainers in my room we'd have got out of the village before the tree came down,' said Amber, back to her usual self.

Mum stormed into the living room, arms crossed, face crosser. 'Cut it out, you two.' She wheezed; a toxic bubble popping faintly somewhere deep inside her.

Ethan understood how bad things had got with Mum, but he was sure that Amber didn't really get it. She was only nine, after all. He was a whole two years older, so it was his job to protect her from things like this.

'Dad's trying to get a signal on his mobile.' Mum drew in a high-pitched keening breath before staring hard at the pair of them. There was instant silence. That stare said it all.

Ethan could tell Amber was on the verge of tears, even though she tried to put on a brave face.

Dad stomped into the living room, waving the mobile phone above his head. 'It's no use, there's no signal anywhere.'

Amber started crying. Quietly at first but building up to huge blubbering sobs. 'Our holiday's ruined and Daddy's car is broken.'

Ethan snapped out of his sullen mood. Amber only ever used the word *"Daddy"* when she was really upset. His little sister could be annoying at times, but he didn't like seeing her cry. That's when he had an idea. Grabbing a hairbrush from her travel bag, he held it up like a microphone and cleared his throat.

'A man takes his Labrador to the vets. He says "My dog's cross-eyed. Is there anything you can do for him?"' "Well, says the vet, let's have a look at him." So he picks the dog up and examines his eyes then checks his teeth. Finally, he says, "I'm going to have to put him down." The owner says "What, because he's cross-eyed?" "No," said the vet, "because he's really heavy."'

Amber threw her hair scrunchy at Ethan, hitting him square in the face. 'That was awful.'

'It took your mind off things, though.' He grinned, throwing the scrunchy back at her.

'Will you two keep the noise down?' shouted Dad, 'I can't hear myself think.'

'Sorry, Dad. I was trying to cheer Amber up a bit.'

'Yes, well. Go and play quietly in the kitchen, or something.'

'Look, It's almost stopped raining,' said Mum. 'Why don't the pair of you pop out to the shed, and have a look at the board games out there while I whip up something cold for lunch.'

'Monopoly,' said Ethan. 'I'm so going to bankrupt you,' he said and giggled as they headed for the back door.

'Yeah, you wish,' said Amber.

Weaving their way around fallen branches and an overturned barbecue grill, they reached the little wooden hut, which was luckily still in one piece.

'How are we going to get in?' Amber stood at the edge of an enormous puddle which had formed right in front of the shed. She pointed at the door. 'Our welly boots are in there.'

Ethan stared at the floating twigs and leaves and thought hard. 'Got it.' He snapped his fingers. 'Give us a hand with these rockery stones.' They soon had a line of steppingstones that reached three quarters of the way across the water. 'Nearly there. If I can just...' With a huge rock cradled in his arms, Ethan tottered over the dirty water. Fighting to keep his balance, he lurched left. The narrow steppingstone he balanced on slid right, and he became airborne. Ethan and the rock parted company. The rock splooshed to the right, and Ethan splashed down to the left.

Amber nimbly side-stepped the wave and stared down. 'I can't believe you just did that.' She chuckled. The sight of her bedraggled brother glaring up at her soon turned the chuckles into gales of hysterical laughter. 'It was much funnier than your rubbish joke.'

Ethan's glare soon became a grin. It *was* funny when he thought about it. Easing himself onto his knees, he felt a bolt of electricity surge through his body, knocking him back into the water. Pin pricks of bright white light danced behind his eyes. It was as if part of the storm had somehow managed to energise the puddle. He looked about, searching for the source of the shock. The overhead cable which connected to the roof of the house was still intact, so what was going on? The second jolt hit him just as he scrambled to his feet. All of his muscles tensed at once, his teeth snapping shut on his tongue.

'What are you doing now, you loony?' Amber managed to say between attacks of mirth. 'Is this some kind of new dance, or something?'

Ethan wasn't sure what it was, but he knew his tongue hurt like crazy, and a weird low hum came from inside his pocket. He dragged himself onto dry land. Fishing in his pocket, his fingers closed on something lumpy and hard. It was the odd-coloured lump of quartz he'd found that morning. What with the storm and the car wreck, he'd forgotten all about it. He stared down at it. It pulsed with a pink light and throbbed a deep rhythmic note. He rubbed his eyes and looked again. No pulsing light came from the quartz, and it definitely wasn't humming. He wasn't sure whether he'd imagined it or not. Did it light up and hum? Or was his mind playing tricks on him? He shook his head slowly and put the crystal back in his pocket.

'What's happened to you?' Dad asked. 'I thought

the rain had stopped.'

'There's a giant puddle by the shed,' said Amber with a giggle, 'and big feet here went and fell in.'

'Shut up, you,' said Ethan.

'It gets worse.' Amber became more and more animated. 'He goes and does this funny little dance, like he was electrocuted, or something.'

'Go on, up to the bathroom and get dried off,' said Dad. 'And no more messing about, all right?'

'It's not as if I wanted to get cold and wet again,' Ethan whined, as he stomped up the stairs.

'Ethan,' called Dad through the bathroom door.

'What?'

'When you've got yourself sorted out, do me a favour and take Amber to the park, will you?'

'What for?' he said, exiting the bathroom.

'Me and your mum are going back to the car to unload, and Amber wants to go on the swings,' said Dad.

'Yeah, so?' Ethan stared at the carpet and jammed his hands deep into his jeans pockets.

'All right. I know the holiday's ruined, but there's no need for that attitude.'

'Whatever,' said Ethan dismissively and headed for the stairs.

Dad's voice rose in volume. 'I'm not asking, young man; you'll do as you're told.'

'I'm going OK! Tell Amber to meet me outside.'

CHAPTER 2

An Unlikely Portal

The park smelled of freshly mown grass, and that clean outdoor smell you get after a summer storm.

'I'm going on the swings,' said Amber.

'Do what you want. Ethan shrugged and shuffled along the boundary path, kicking at small stones. He couldn't help feeling he'd been a little mean to Amber, but sometimes she just deserved it. Why did he always have to do exactly what she wanted, all the time? It wasn't fair.

His forehead hurt. Putting his hand up to massage the pain, he noticed there were deep crease lines. He must have been frowning for so long, it had given him a headache.

'What's up with you, misery guts?'

He had reached the swings where Amber was playing and hadn't noticed. 'Oh hi, Amber,' he said absently, glancing up as she soared skywards. 'I've been thinking. Back in the garden when I fell in that puddle, I had a really weird feeling.'

Amber brought the swing to a halt, her boots sending up a hail of gravel. 'Yeah, of course you did. It was embarrassment because you landed face down in it.'

Ethan glared at her. 'I'm being serious, so just listen, OK? This morning I found something after Jimmy had been digging in the garden.' He pulled the pink quartz out of his pocket, sunlight glinting off the golden flecks. Amber hopped off the swing to get a closer look.

'What is it?'

'I think it's quartz,' said Ethan. 'When I fell in the puddle, it started to hum and pulse with a strange light.' The crystal shard sat in his palm silent and definitely unlit.

'What do you mean, is it alien, or something?' she said with a smirk.

'I don't know, but it gave me a couple of nasty shocks.'

Amber's face lit up with a huge grin. 'Zapped by aliens who want their moon rock back. Just wait till I tell Jessica at school. Locate the Tardis and exterminate.' Arms outstretched, Amber performed a stiff legged robot walk around the swings, before dissolving into helpless laughter. Ethan ignored her and stomped off. As he headed towards the playing fields, a large puddle caught his eye. An image flashed across its surface that wasn't a reflection of anything in the park. Curiosity got the better of him, and he edged closer to get a better look. An unearthly greenish yellow glow shone from the small pool of water, as if the puddle had lit up from underneath. The entrance to a strange underground world swam into view. Vast crystals jutted from a huge black lake. Enormous columns of rock towered above the cave floor like prehistoric skyscrapers. 'Waah!' He leaped backwards, landing with a splatch on the waterlogged grass. Heart pounding, he edged forward until he stood directly over the water. Looking down again, all he could see was muddy water and tarmac. Where had the cave entrance gone? Shaking his head and rubbing his eyes, he looked again. Nothing. What was going on? First that weird pink crystal goes off on one, and now there's a massive cave in a puddle in the park. Or was there? It was just a puddle, after all, not deep enough to float a duck. As he turned away, he glanced over his shoulder at the little pool one last time. To his amazement, he saw the other world shining out of the puddle in all its glory. The stacks of weird glowing rocks, the huge crystals and the massive black lake were real. It wasn't a figment of his imagination, after all. The pink quartz in his pocket thrummed madly. He pulled it out to check it. The pulsing light was now so bright it made his eyes hurt. He stuffed the shard back into his jeans and sped across the playground to where Amber was attempting a swing-powered moon launch.

'Amber, I've got to show you something.' He skidded to a stop in front of her soaring feet.

'Get out of the way, or you'll get kicked in the face! Her boots whooshed past his ear.

'Just listen for a sec. I've just seen something well weird.'

Amber launched herself off the swing as it arced upwards. Long hair flying like a blonde flag, she sailed gracefully through the air before landing lightly on the tarmac path.

'You've got to come with me. I have to show you the magic cave. The crystal too, it's going nuts. Come on, hurry.'

'Slow down, I can't understand a word you're saying. Tell me again, but slowly this time.'

Ethan took a deep breath. 'This is serious. I have to show you something important.' Fighting to keep his voice under control, he told Amber about the strange puddle cave.

'I always knew you were loopy,' muttered Amber, as she trailed behind her impatient brother.

'Stand there, turn around, and look over your shoulder directly into the puddle.' Amber did as Ethan requested, but all there was to see was a pool of dirty water. The pink and gold crystal also stayed stubbornly dark and silent, no matter what Ethan did with it. He waved it around as if trying to get a signal on a cell phone. There was no humming or glowing this time. It was just a piece of colourful rock with no magical abilities whatsoever.

'I'm bored,' said Amber. 'I'll be on the slide if you want me.'

'Please don't go,' he begged her. 'I'm not making it up.'

'Give me a hand would you, Ethan.' Back at the house, Dad tried to wheel a suitcase up the front steps, but the handle had broken at one end, causing the case to flop over onto one side.

'Yeah, all right. If I have to.'

'I see your mood hasn't lightened up,' said Dad, as he hefted the case into the hallway.

'It's because he reckons he saw some kind of magic cave in a puddle in the park,' said Amber. 'He's got a lump of moon rock, as well. He says the cat dug it up.'

Ethan glared at his sister. 'Shut up, and leave me alone!' he shouted, before stomping off through the lounge.

'What's up, Ethan?' Mum looked worried. 'Are you coming down with something?'

'I'm fine,' he grumbled. 'I'm going to my room.' Slamming the bedroom door behind him, he threw himself onto the bed. Staring at the ceiling, he thought hard about the pink crystal and the strange puddle cave. The crystal and the cave were connected somehow. The quartz lit up and hummed when the cave appeared. There was no way it was coincidental. The intermittent sunshine cast lengthening shadows across the ceiling, as the hours slid by. Ethan kept turning over the events in his head, coming back every time to the same conclusion. He had to go back to the park. Leaping out of bed, he pulled open the door, jamming his foot against it, forcing it shut again. The slam was hard enough to rattle his framed swimming certificates.

'Ethan!' Dad's irritated voice boomed from downstairs. 'What are you doing up there? Keep the racket down, will you!'

'I'm going to the park for a kick about,' he lied. How could he explain to his father that he was searching for a magic puddle cave?

'I'll come with you.' Amber emerged from her bedroom and pulled on her fleece.

'Bog off, Amber. I'm going to play football.' She'd laughed at him when he'd fallen in the puddle, and that niggled him. Worse still was when he saw the puddle cave. It was there. He'd seen it. But she wouldn't believe him, *and* she'd made fun of him in front of Dad. 'I don't want you hanging around.' He headed for the stairs when she piped up.

'You forgot your ball.'

Dark simmering resentment bubbled just below the surface, but Ethan pushed it back down.

'Oh yeah, right,' he muttered and turned to grab the ball from his bedroom floor.

'I'm going to the park with Ethan,' said Amber, as she ran down the stairs.

'No way. I'm going to meet a friend.' Why did she insist on following him everywhere? Didn't she have a life of her own? 'I've taken you to the park already, so just leave me alone.'

The living room door opened, and Dad stuck his head out. 'I heard that.' He pointed a finger at Ethan. 'Take your sister to the park with you and don't argue.'

'But...'

'No buts,' said Dad. 'Go on. I'll see the pair of you in a couple of hours.'

'Why don't you go and play with Jessica, instead of hassling me?' Ethan sat on the ball with his chin in his hands. 'I'm sick of you hanging about.' A heavy blanket of dark thoughts smothered Ethan's good humour, and any happiness he may have had now lay smouldering like a damp bonfire. He didn't quite know what he was feeling. Misery, resentment, anger? He just knew he had an overwhelming urge to unleash the rage. 'Get out of my sight, you stupid girl!'

Unfortunately, Amber was in the firing line. She backed away from his onslaught, head tilted in a "why?" gesture.

'I sometimes wish you'd never been born!' He bellowed, spittle showering her face. Instant regret burned him like a hot knife, but the momentum of his wrath was unrelenting. 'You're nothing but...but...' The words stuck in his throat as he glared up at his sister.

'Why are you being so horrible?' she said. 'Sometimes I wish...' A mix of emotions flashed across her face. Confusion, anger, pain and a deep sense of hurt.

He knew he had broken something precious, but at that moment he didn't care. If he could take back the last few minutes, would he? Fury and guilt battled to gain the upper hand. He turned away from Amber, snatched up his ball and stomped across the park.

The stormy weather had passed. The heavy humid air of the past few weeks had been replaced by a far crisper feel. The deluge had left an autumnal snap in the air, even though it was almost a whole week until September.

Ethan got as far as the rocket shaped climbing frame when he stopped and looked down. At his feet was a large muddy puddle. He stared at it and thought about the vision he had only a few hours earlier. There's no way it could be real. Magic disappearing caves? Yeah, right! He stepped around the water. Just before he strode off across the playing field, he glanced down one more time. Dropping the ball, heart missing a beat, he stared into the magic cave. There it was again. He hadn't imagined it after all. The black lake, the huge crystals, and the massive rock formations weren't all in his head, after all. The quartz in his pocket suddenly sprang back to life, humming harder than ever. He plunged a hand into his jeans and pulled out the vibrating rock. The unearthly pink light had got stronger and pulsed much faster. 'Amber!'

He sprinted the short distance to the slide. 'It's come back. The magic cave in the puddle. It's come back. You've got to come with me before it vanishes again.'

'I'm not talking to you.' Amber huffed and glided gracefully down the slide.

Ethan knew he'd hurt her, but it just didn't seem important right now.

He grabbed her by the hand and almost pulled her off her feet as he headed back towards the climbing frame.

'Look.' He pointed at the small muddy pool.

'What am I looking at?' said Amber. 'There's nothing there.'

Ethan stared at the puddle and then back at Amber. 'It really was there,' he said weakly. 'I know it was. And this pink and gold quartz went mad.'

'It's you that's gone mad.' Amber turned to walk away. She glanced over her shoulder and was about to say something else when the sun broke through the clouds.

'What's wrong?' Ethan followed her gaze, and there it was, the magic cave, just like before. At that moment, the pink crystal in his hand lit up like a spotlight and vibrated so hard, he almost dropped it. 'I told you, didn't I?' Ethan ran to the edge of the puddle. 'There's something down there. I know you can see it too!' shouted Ethan, whilst Amber stood gaping, open-mouthed at the vision shining from the water. 'I said I wasn't making it up, and this crystal thing, I think it's got something to do with it.' Pulsing lighthouse bright, the pink rock throbbed with an intensity that made it difficult to hold on to. The sparkling sunlight glittered on the surface of the water as Amber glanced nervously between the flashing rock and the eerie looking portal.

'Wha... what is it?' She tilted her head left and right. 'It's like one of those 3D hologram pictures. It can't be real though, can it?' Backing away from the portal, she took hold of Ethan's wrist. 'I don't like it; I think we should go home. That crystal thing too, I don't think you should hold it anymore.'

Ethan stared into the glowing world below. 'It's amazing.' He pulled free from Amber's grip, eyes wide. 'It's a whole other universe in a puddle.'

'I'm going to get Mummy and Daddy. Come on, let's go.' Amber tugged at Ethan's wrist once more.

'Just let me have a closer look.' Ethan shook her off and shuffled as close to the edge of the water as he could, without touching it. 'I can make out some more details. If I can just lean over a bit more, I'll be able to...'

The glowing rock in his right hand jolted violently, causing him to lean out much further than he aimed to. His world spun through a hundred and eighty degrees. The sky became the ground as his trainers lost their grip on the muddy grass. Arms outstretched, he hurtled into the puddle. Instead of landing in a crumpled heap on the playground path, he passed through the shallow pool as though it was a liquid doorway. Screwing his eyes shut, he braced himself for a long drop and at the very least, broken arms and legs when he hit the bottom. Thankfully, he only fell a short distance and landed with a splat in a small pool of icy water. Opening his eyes, he could see the bottom of the puddle six feet or so above him. He could also see the world beyond. It was like looking through the bottom of a fish tank. There was the climbing frame, there was the cloudy blue sky, and there was his sister frantically waving her arms and screaming at him. Staggering to his feet, he stared up into Amber's face. 'Go and get help. Get Mum and Dad. They'll know what to do.'

Amber mouthed the word 'what?' He realised he couldn't hear her, and by the looks of it, she couldn't hear him, either. What he could hear, though, was the constant sound of dripping water and a low rumbling roar like some enormous wild animal. He had fallen into the puddle portal, and unless Amber went for help, he was trapped there. Looking down, he found himself standing on a high narrow ledge that sloped away at an alarming angle in all directions. He was perched on one of those huge stone skyscrapers his teacher called a stalagmite. He peered over the edge, instantly regretting it. There was a vast cavern below, lit by an eerie greenish yellow glow. The enormous crystalline shapes he'd seen earlier jutted from a smooth black lake. His head swam, causing him to

overbalance, and before he knew what was happening, he plummeted down the face of the rock,
headfirst.

CHAPTER 3

Puddlemere

He tumbled over and over, arms thrashing and legs furiously peddling empty air. The smooth black surface of the lake exploded outwards as he plunged through it. Limbs still pumping, he churned up the water, coughing and spluttering as he tried not to drown. Dragging himself onto the shore, he flopped down, panting, wheezing and spitting out icy metallic tasting water. He sucked in lungfuls of air that smelled of damp earth after a rainstorm, mingled with a sharp chemical tang. As his breathing started to ease, he sat up. He wiggled his fingers and toes. Relieved nothing was broken, he reached for his phone which came out of his pocket in about thirty pieces, broken glass and bits of casing clattering to the ground. That was the end of his emergency call. Getting to his feet, he looked around, checking his surroundings. The vision before him was breath-taking. Vast crystals jutted out of the black surface of the lake. Spiky shards of green and red stabbed the air, giving off a luminous glare that touched everything around him.

All along the shoreline strange rock formations stood guard like a fossilised army. Looking to his left, he discovered the source of the thunderous roar. In the distance he could see an enormous waterfall cascading over immense rubies and emeralds. The spray filled the air with a fine mist and would have soaked him if he wasn't already half drowned. Draining his trainers, he set off in the direction of the waterfall and had just started walking when a feeling of unease seized him. He glanced around, wiping both hands on his trousers. Nothing. He mustn't let his imagination run away with him. Laughing nervously to himself, he continued on. He'd gone no more than a dozen paces when a sudden movement in the lake caught his eye, pulling him up short. Peering out across the water, he was sure he could see a face amongst a cluster of dark green crystals. He stared through the mist until his eyes started watering. Deciding he was imagining things, he shook his head and set off once more.

A ripple broke the smooth surface of the water. This time he was sure. The face was real, and this time it looked up at him from the surface of the lake. Without taking his eyes from the water, Ethan backed away until he bumped into one of the rock soldiers. He turned to run but time had slowed to a near stop. His heart must have been hammering, but all he could feel was a deep b-boom resonating in his chest. His palms suddenly felt cold. He'd forgotten he was soaked to the skin. His waterlogged jeans weighed on him, holding him back as his feet gradually picked up the pace. If he could find somewhere to hide, get away from that weird head, he'd have a chance to gather his thoughts and figure out a way to escape. His lungs burned as he pushed on towards the falls. There it was, a gap. There was a ledge running along the cliff, and it tucked in behind the waterfall. If he could ease himself in behind the torrent, he'd never be spotted.

The wall of water was big, and as he slid to a stop, he realised how big. Pictures he'd seen of Niagara Falls popped into his frazzled mind as he gawped up at the gigantic wall of white water. It let out an unending earth-shaking roar, pushing his senses into overload. The fine mist was now a cloud billowing around the base of the falls, making it difficult for him to see.

A piece of the waterfall slid sideways across Ethan's vision. He stared in numb disbelief. An ice sculpture of a man stepped from the frothing spume, but it wasn't ice, it couldn't be. Water ran over ice, not through it. A deep chill ran through Ethan, and he took an involuntary step backwards. Water isn't supposed to move like that. It can dance, he'd seen fountains. But it can't walk. It can't smile. A living pond stood before him. Arms, legs, body, head. A man as clear as a glass of water was holding out a hand for him to shake. Ethan's arms hung limp by his side as he looked from the glistening fingers to the see-through head. Bloated jowls framed a smile that almost, but not quite reached a pair of piercing liquid eyes. Thinning blue hair was scraped back across a watery scalp and pulled into a lank ponytail.

'My name is Storm Floodwater. You must be an Overlander.' The sounds of falling rain, pattering April showers and waves washing a shingle beach flowed together to form the voice of the watery being. 'It's extremely rare to see an Overlander in Puddlemere. There must be a shift in the parallel planes of existence.'

'What's Puddlemere?' Ethan's voice bordered on stuttering, his mind playing catch-up with his eyes.

'Puddlemere? You're standing in it. It's the elemental plane of water. I am a water elemental, and this is my home.'

The water-being appeared to be cheerful and fairly likeable.

'Why did you call me an Overlander?' Questions kept popping into Ethan's mind.

'Because you come from a *land* which is situated *over* the top of ours, hence Overland. I take it you do have a name?'

Ethan thought about giving him a made-up name but decided against it. 'Myles. Ethan Myles, and I need to get back home. Like now.'

'Well, Myles Ethan Myles, in order to get you home, I first need to take you to the ruby palace to meet his watery majesty, Emperor Monsoon. Hop onto my back and hold on tight. We'll be there in no time.'

Ethan's eyes narrowed. 'Why do I need to go and see your emperor? I just want to go home, and all I need is a little help to climb back up that stalagmite. From there, I can get back through the puddle and into the park where my sister's waiting for me.'

Storm Floodwater knelt down in front of Ethan. 'You have a sister?'

Ethan frowned. 'Err, yes. Why?'

Storm Floodwater shook his head. 'No matter. The important thing is, I cannot help you on my own as the stalagmite is far too big. The emperor can order a battalion of troops to build a ladder for you to climb to the top.'

Ethan sifted through the information. Yes, the stalagmite was huge, and it would be difficult to climb with only one person helping. A battalion of guards would make sense, as they could carry the supplies for the ladder and build it in no time at all.

'Well?' Storm Floodwater looked questioningly at Ethan. 'Do you want my help, or not?'

Ethan thought it over for a few more seconds. 'How do I know you're telling the truth?'

'That's a good question and one that only you can answer. Do you leave here on the back of a stranger you've never met before? Or do you stay here on your own and pray someone from Overland can find a way to rescue you? Before you starve to death, of course.'

Putting it like that, Ethan realised he only had one option. He'd have to go with Storm Floodwater and hope he was as good as his word. 'OK, bend forward a little so I can climb onto your back.' Ethan tried to sound braver than he felt. The water-being's skin felt really odd. It was like holding onto solid water. Hard like a person but at the same time, as liquid as a puddle of rain.

'Hold on tight.' Storm Floodwater walked out onto the surface of the lake and sunk down, until only his top half was visible above the shiny blackness. Ethan gripped his companion's shoulders as they sped through a network of caves. Glittering diamond-like crystals and glowing white columns of rock whizzed past in a blur. Jutting shapes of emeralds, the size of double-decker buses, sprouted from radiant yellow rocks. Ethan was sure he spotted faces peering at him from the giant gemstones as he zipped by them. On and on they travelled through the alien landscape, until a cluster of the biggest rubies Ethan had ever seen came into view. Sitting on an island in the middle of a cathedral-sized cavern was the ruby palace. As amazing as the structure was, all Ethan could think about was the fact that he would soon be going home.

Storm Floodwater slowed to a gentle stop in

front of the palace, and Ethan climbed down. Bone thin flying buttresses of glittering red crystal supported finely carved towers. Hexagonal turrets soared upwards into the darkness above, topped by steep conical spires. Long crimson pennants snapped in the continual warm breeze that blew through the huge chamber. The entire structure seemed to be carved from one giant ruby. The path leading to the entrance was paved with ruby tiles that led to a pair of ornate gates. Vertical bars of deep crimson were topped with a dazzling array of diamonds and emeralds, which spelt out the letters E and M. Ethan couldn't help thinking he was in Oz. Maybe the wrong colour though. As they reached the entrance, Ethan noticed a pair of guards dressed in bright red uniforms.

'Sergeant Floodwater, you're late back from patrol!'

The soldiers looked as though they'd stepped out of a picture on an old-fashioned chocolate box. The only difference being their see-through heads.

'And what's this creature you've brought back with you?'

The nearest guard marched towards Storm Floodwater, his waxed moustache quivering as he bellowed in his face.

'I am your superior officer, and when I ask a question, you answer!'

Storm Floodwater snapped to attention. 'Yes, Master Chief, sir! I have discovered an Overlander, sir. Whilst patrolling the Silver Ponds area. It wishes to return to its own world, sir.'

The officer leaned in to get a closer look at Ethan. Unlike Storm, this soldier had a short purple fringe and long whiskery sideburns that framed a hard, uncompromising face.

'Hmm, it wants to return to its own world, eh?' The officer straightened up and turned to face Storm Floodwater. 'Very well, I order you to escort our *guest* to the throne room ante-chamber. If this truly is an Overlander, I'll need to discuss the possibility of it having the recipe Doctor Freeze has been searching for. You will then await further instructions. Do I make myself clear, Floodwater?'

Storm Floodwater saluted. 'Crystal, sir.'

Worry gnawed at the corners of Ethan's mind as he was led through the gates and into the vast carved ruby. What was this recipe they wanted? He couldn't even boil an egg.

The throne room antechamber was also red, as Ethan expected it would be. A plush scarlet carpet covered the floor. Red and gold tapestries depicting water elementals riding tentacled sea monsters hung from maroon picture rails.

'Make yourself at home. I'll be right back.' Ethan didn't like the way Storm Floodwater grinned at him. It just seemed *off* somehow. He was about to take a seat on the uncomfortable looking sofa when a noise stopped him cold. It was a loud clunk. The sound of a door being locked.

CHAPTER 4

The Ruby Palace

I t took Ethan a while to grasp his situation. He was in a parallel world of water elementals, and they thought he had some sort of recipe they wanted. Gripping the intricately carved door handle, he gave it a turn. Nothing. Well, what did he expect? It niggled him as to why Storm Floodwater wanted to know about Amber. He wished he hadn't mentioned her now. He didn't like the sound of this Doctor Freeze, either. He paced soundlessly on the thick carpet as he tried to figure out what to do next. The door had been locked, so whatever it was these beings wanted, they didn't want him to escape.

He had to get out of there. He pulled out his house keys and jiggled one of them in the lock trying to pick it, but of course it was no use. The hanging tapestries didn't hide any hidden exits or secret passages. He tried to lift the sofa to see if it covered any trapdoors. It was so heavy he couldn't budge it. Not even by a millimetre. He was so pre-occupied trying to prise up the rug, that when the lock clicked, he didn't even notice. The door swung inwards, making a whishing sound over the thick carpet.

'Myles Ethan Myles.' Ethan jumped. He leapt to his feet, banging his head on the arm of the bur-gundy sofa.

'Wha... what?' He rubbed his forehead and stared at Storm Floodwater who had returned with two more soldiers. Each guard was armed with a strange looking pistol. A wooden handle con-nected to a polished copper ball, on top of which was some sort of light bulb in a protective cage. The bulb throbbed rhythmically with a weak yellow light. The short black barrel puffed out a thin stream of white vapour in time with the pulsing bulb, and each weapon pointed directly at him.

Storm Floodwater cleared his throat and un-rolled an official looking document. 'His immor-tal imperial majesty, Emperor Monsoon, has so ordered he be presented with the Overlander, one Myles Ethan Myles, forthwith.'

The two guards stepped into the room and seized Ethan firmly by the arms, giving him no time to react. His shock at being grabbed gave way to a worrying sense of doom. He was being taken to meet the emperor as promised, but why under armed guard?

'Private Drizzle, Private Drip!' barked Storm Floodwater. 'Escort our guest to the throne room. By the left, quick march!'

Struggling was less than pointless, so Ethan just allowed the water men to drag him through the wide crystal corridors.

The two guards on patrol stood to attention as Ethan was led through a dazzling ruby archway. Cherubs surfing carved crystal waves looked down on him with glassy stares as he stumbled up the dais steps towards the emperor.

'So, you're Myles Ethan Myles from Overland, then.' Shallow sunlit brooks chattering over glistening pebbles formed the youthful voice which belied the emperor's years. The long angular face had grooves deep enough to fall into, and silver laced the thick blue plait that ran the length of his back. He was clothed entirely in blood red gems, knitted together with fine gold thread that twinkled when he moved.

'I am told by Puddlemere's senior scientist, Doctor Freeze, that humans have the unique ability to create fun.' He leaned in close enough for Ethan to see the individual diamonds that studded the golden rim of his monocle. 'This in turn makes you my new best friend.' His sharp features softened as he patted Ethan's head.

The emperor's soothing voice had an underlying edge to it that put Ethan on his guard. He flinched under the liquid touch, his nerves zinging, causing his throat to constrict.

'Create fun?' His voice was not much more than a squeak. He coughed, playing for time. 'I'm not sure I follow.' He glanced around. The throne room was long and narrow and ended in a wall decorated with carved ruby waves. If he made a break for it, he couldn't go that way. No exit. Go back? Guards were behind him. He wouldn't get more than three paces. He swallowed hard and looked up at the emperor.

'Now don't be modest.' The emperor's face rippled as if a stone had been dropped into a pond. 'You're a very special boy. You have a sense of fun so highly developed and so finely tuned, the fun machine's readings were off the chart. All I need from you is the recipe, and I will arrange for your safe return home.'

Ethan frowned in confusion. 'What's a fun machine?'

The emperor stood up and took a step towards him, his voice dropping to a near whisper. 'The fun machine is none of your concern, but I will tell you something that is. You came into Puddlemere through a puddle. When the puddle dries out, you will never see your world again. Do I make myself clear?'

Ethan stared up at the emperor. What was this all about? Something called a fun machine, a recipe he was supposed to know, and now the puddle he fell through will become a one-way ticket if it dries out. 'What? I have to get home. Please, I...I...'

The emperor cut him off. 'Search him, and then escort him to the ruby dungeons,' he said to Storm Floodwater.

'Yes, your Eminence.' The water man patted Ethan down, and when he reached his jeans pocket, he stopped. 'What have we got here?' He held the pink crystal up to the light.

The emperor's eyes went wide. 'The missing rose gold quartz. How did you come by this?'

'It was in the garden,' said Ethan. 'My cat dug it up.'

'You mean to tell me that one of my rose gold quartz crystals just popped up in your garden from nowhere? You expect me to believe *that*? Tell me Myles Ethan Myles, how did you steal it?'

'Steal it? I didn't steal it.' Ethan's voice trembled as the emperor paced to and fro in front of him.

'Who are your Puddlemere contacts? Why would humans need rose gold quartz? Answer me!'

Ethan felt the strength drain out of his legs as the emperor continued his interrogation.

'Our fun was stolen by your people on Black Funday!' Droplets of hot water sprayed from the emperor's mouth and splashed steaming onto the floor. 'You have the finest fun essence I've ever seen, but I need you to tell me how you made it!' Watery fists slammed down onto the arms of the ruby throne, as the sound of a hurricane driven wave ricocheted around the huge chamber. He approached Ethan at an alarming pace, forcing him to tumble back into the arms of Storm Flood-water. Gripping Ethan's wrists, Storm pushed him towards the emperor. 'Tell me what I need to know!' Emperor Monsoon bellowed. 'When that puddle dries out, you'll be stuck here forever!'

Ethan stared up at the emperor, whose face was so close to his own, their noses almost touched. Tinged red by the crimson glow of the palace, the emperor seemed almost demonic.

'Tick tock, Myles Ethan Myles.'

Ethan fought hard to stop the tears that pricked the corners of his eyes from escaping. He didn't want this monstrous creature to see how upset he was. Try as he might, though, he couldn't hold back any longer. Dragging in huge lungfuls of air between sobs, he tried to speak but only managed a hiccup.

The emperor prodded him in the chest with a watery finger. 'Enough with this sniffling. It occurs to me that all the information I need is locked in your brain. Doctor Freeze tells me that Overlanders have solid brains, and all thoughts, knowledge and ideas are stored there.' He rapped Ethan twice on the head as though he was knocking on a door. 'He also assures me that the information I need can be retrieved, and all I have to do is have that marvellous recording device of yours removed and disassembled.' Turning to face Storm Floodwater, the emperor uttered words so chilling, they stopped Ethan's sobs and turned his tears to ice. 'Sergeant Floodwater.'

Storm clicked his heels together. 'Yes, your Majesty.'

'Take the prisoner to the ruby dungeons and alert Doctor Freeze. Tell him to prepare the specimen for dissection.'

'Right away, your greatness.' Storm Floodwater grabbed Ethan by the shoulders and dragged him towards the exit.

'Dissection? You're going to dissect me like a lab rat?' Panic took over as his heart jumped in his chest. 'OK, I'll tell you everything. I'll give you the recipe. I'll tell you the names of the spies I'm in contact with. There's no need to dice me up.'

Emperor Monsoon stared unblinkingly at Ethan for a long moment before speaking. 'Don't worry, it won't hurt much. You almost won't feel a thing. Take him away.'

Ethan turned to face Storm Floodwater. 'You said you were my friend. You promised to help get me back home.'

Ignoring his outburst, Storm Floodwater hauled Ethan through the palace corridors down into the bowels of the earth. Inquisitive faces appeared at doorways to gawp at the stranger. They passed state rooms with long moonstone tables glowing with an eerie brilliance and emerald chandeliers the size of small family cars. More water people appeared, to see what the commotion was about. Ethan felt like a new exhibit at London Zoo. As they travelled deeper towards the dungeons, the magnificence gave way to plain rock corridors and functional rooms. The walls were lined with servants quarters, pantries and storerooms. They passed kitchens that emitted a sharp chemical tang that burned Ethan's nostrils and made his eyes stream. There were no curious faces down here. Just a jailer and his prisoner. The further down they went, the darker and greyer it became. Everything around them seemed devoid of colour, which perfectly matched Ethan's mood.

'Welcome to your new home.' Storm Floodwater kicked open a dull grey door. A dollop of sickly smelling green slime dropped from the ceiling with pinpoint accuracy onto the back of Ethan's neck. 'Don't get too comfy. Doctor Freeze will be along soon to collect you for dissecting. And just to think, I was the one who discovered you. I'll get a medal for this.' His captor slammed the heavy granite door with a loud thunk.

CHAPTER 5

Lake Splashdown

E than beat on the door. He kicked it and pulled it. He punched it. Then he wished he hadn't. He yelled and screamed until his voice was no more than a rasping squeak. As his panic lessened, he started to think. The cell looked like a natural cave somebody had put a door on, and as his eyes got used to the dark, he could make out some details. The low rough ceiling sloped away to the rear. Thinking back to his geography class got his brain working. Caves were created by water, and the water has to flow downhill. If he could find where the water flowed away to, he could find a way out. He crawled to the back of the cave to where the ceiling reached down to the floor. If the water got out that way, the gap was way too small for him to fit. He scrambled back to the middle of the room. His mind drifted to thoughts of the emperor. 'He thinks humans stole the Puddle peoples' fun,' he said to the empty cell. 'And I've got the secret to its creation locked in my head. That's the maddest thing I've ever heard. These beings are insane. What sort of lunatics dissect kids?' Panic ignited once again, burning brightly enough to blot out rational thought. 'Help me, help me!' he croaked, his voice no more than a scratchy whisper.

'Keep the noise down.'

Ethan wheeled around, bashing his head on a low-hanging piece of rock. 'Huh, who's there?' He frantically scanned the small room. Nothing.

'I'm coming in now, so don't scream.' The voice came from under the floor. Ethan backed towards the door, eyes darting over the rough surface. A section of rock shifted ever so slightly. Ethan's heart galloped in his chest. He was about to be dissected. Were these his last few moments? Time slowed and a single bead of cold sweat traced a path down his face. Ignoring the salt sting as it reached his eye, he took another backward step. The door felt cool as he pressed his hands against it. He'd gone as far as he could. The only thing left for him to do now was to fight.

A slab of granite about the size of a manhole cover slowly started to rise. Ethan's fingernails dug grooves into his palms as he tightened his fists ready for action. His head swam at the thought of fighting. He was never any good at it and would always come off worse. Crouching low and staring through sweat stung eyes, he watched as a wide brimmed leather hat appeared through the hole.

'Myles Ethan Myles?'

This wasn't a palace guard. He wasn't wearing a uniform. The neatly trimmed goatee beard and pointed moustache reminded him of the three musketeers, only shorter.

'Who are you?'

'My name is Lake Splashdown. We both have to get out of here, right away.'

It all felt wrong, somehow. This miniature version of D'Artagnan with his buckled boots wasn't much taller than him, but he felt dangerous. Feral cat dangerous. It looks like a house cat, but you know that if you mess with it, you'll end up hospitalised. 'You're here to take me to be dissected, aren't you?'

The mini musketeer gripped Ethan by the arm. 'No, I'm not, actually.'

Ethan wriggled free from the water man's grip. Dangerous or not, he had no choice but to fight or die. His knuckles crunched against Lake's jaw snapping his head round.

'Steady on, I'm here to rescue you.'

'That's what the other one said and look where I ended up!' Ethan threw another punch, striking out with his right hand. As quick as Ethan was, Lake Splashdown was quicker. He seemed to flow to one side, then his hand shot out and grabbed Ethan's wrist.

'Have you quite finished trying to kill your rescuer? Will you just..? Lake Splashdown stopped talking as Ethan's forehead collided with his nose. 'Oh, that's gonna hurt.' The elemental grabbed his nose, before transforming into a column of spinning water. Ethan jumped back as the whirlpool closed in on him. 'Settle down and listen for a second.' Lake's voice came from somewhere deep inside the vortex. 'I'm on your side.'

'I don't believe you!' screeched Ethan, as he charged head long at the whirling Lake Splashdown. There was a blur of liquid feet and a feeling of weightlessness as Ethan left the floor. The air left his lungs with a whoosh, as he hit the stony ground with a flump. Pain stabbed the length of his spine.

'Are you done now? We haven't got time for all of this fuss.'

Ethan looked up at Lake's face through a sea of popping stars. The elemental had transformed back into person-shape and held out a hand.

'We've got to go before that maniac Doctor Freeze arrives.'

The fight had gone out of Ethan, and knowing he was beaten, offered his hand to be helped up.

'I lead a secret organisation called the Dryads. We are opposed to Emperor Monsoon and his followers. And as for Doctor Freeze, well, he's just plain evil,' said Lake Splashdown, hauling Ethan to his feet. Ethan headed for the hole in the ground, hoping this time it was the right choice. As he lunged forward in the hope of escaping, his canoe sized trainer clipped the edge of the rock manhole cover. The loose lump of stone slid along the damp floor and settled back into its hole with a clump.

Lake sunk to the floor. 'You five-star idiot. Go to the top of the class. Now that we're both locked in, let me slap you on the back and congratulate you. When Freeze and the guards arrive any second now, they'll have you to dissect, and me to execute. Considering I'm a wanted outcast, they'll be delighted to see me here, as well.'

'You were really going to rescue me, then?' The reality of the situation settled in Ethan's mind. Not only had he wasted valuable time by attacking his rescuer, he'd blocked the escape route by kicking the slab back into the hole. What had he done?

Lake glared at him. 'Bravo! The Puddlemere mastermind championship goes to... Myles Ethan, *I finally get it,* Myles.'

'Shut up, will you. I didn't ask to be here.' Ethan studied the lump of stone. The loose slab had slotted into its hole so perfectly, it was difficult to see where the floor ended, and the slab began. 'I think I can see the rim. Trouble is, I can't even get my door key to fit into the gap to prise it up.' Ethan fiddled with his key ring when Lake Splashdown held up a transparent hand.

'Shh! I can hear voices.' Lake slid over to the door and pressed an ear to it. 'The guards are coming. Quick, show me where the edge is.'

'It's an interesting process. You can attend the dissection if you wish. I'm sure his Imperial Majesty won't object.' The sounds of cracking ice, freezing pipes and deep winter wind joined together to form a jagged cold voice.

Ethan glanced towards the door, then back at Lake Splashdown. 'Is that...?'

'Doctor Freeze, yes. So come on, get that lid off!'

The frigid voice sliced into Ethan's mind as effectively as any scalpel. He'd never heard anything so utterly devoid of warmth.

'Well, hurry up and open this door. I've an important operation to perform. I haven't got all day.'

The icy voice of Doctor Freeze rose in volume as jangling keys hit the floor.

'Sor, sorry doctor.' A second voice drifted from the passageway.

'Not to worry, Private Drizzle. Here, let me help you.' Screams erupted from outside the small cell.

'Why do they send me such incompetent fools? Never mind. The hyperthermium should focus your thoughts.'

Ethan frowned at Lake. 'What's...?'

Lake shot an impatient look at Ethan. 'Later. Just keep working.'

Ethan gripped his door key with sweat slicked fingers. The voice. That horrible voice had dug into his brain and was busily shredding his confidence with every Arctic word. With a shaking hand, he slid the key into a tiny gap and twisted as Lake's watery fingers grabbed the edge of the slab.

'You there.' The frozen voice crackled with malice.

'Yes, doctor,' came the nervous reply.

'What's your name, soldier?'

'Private Drip, sir.'

'Well, Drip. I need you to pick up those keys and open the door now!' A wave of frigid air blasted under the gap in the cell door, dropping the temperature several degrees.

Ethan looked up and the key slipped out of his grasp, causing the slab to slot back into its hole with a clunk. He'd done it again. He'd blown their only chance of escape. His breath misted in the cold air, fogging his vision. He had to do this. He had to get it right. Dying was about as bad as it got, or so he thought. Dying a slow death whilst watching somebody cut your brain out was worse. Much worse. Breathing hard and sweating in spite of the cold, he bit down on his fear and jammed the small key into the tiny fissure once again.

The sound of rattling keys floated in on the icy breeze. There was a gentle click. Needle sharp fingers of blue-white ice slid along the door's edge with a screech and Doctor Freeze stepped into the room. The sweat froze on Ethan's face as he looked up at the frost-bound monstrosity. The doctor had the appearance of an ice sculpture that had gone horribly wrong. Spiky icicles jutted out from his face like an explosion of water which had suddenly frozen. Cold blue eyes glared around him with an angry stare. His long slim fingers ended in lethal points. The guards exchanged worried looks. Lake Splashdown looked up as the doctor stared down. Silence fell as their eyes locked.

CHAPTER 6

A Narrow Escape

Time had been distilled down to that one moment. The clocks had been stopped, the Earth had ceased turning, and Ethan stared from Lake to the doctor. This was it, the end. The two elementals just stared at each other until Lake shattered the silence, breaking the spell. 'Move it!' He yanked the lid off the hole.

Ethan didn't need to be told twice and dived head-long into the rock tunnel. He plummeted down a near-vertical shaft into the black depths as Doctor Freeze screeched overhead.

'Bring them back, dead or alive!'

Ethan felt an overwhelming sense of panic well up inside him as he shot into the pitch darkness. As he twisted and sloshed from side to side, a watery hand gripped his ankle. 'Whaa, get off me!' Kicking out hard, Ethan's foot connected with something almost, but not quite solid. With a gurgling whoosh, the hand released its grip and melted into the shadows. The tunnel snaked this way and that, throwing a dizzy Ethan in all directions. What little light there was had now been sucked out completely. It was so dark, he couldn't tell if his eyes were open or shut. That's when a soft *phut* sounded from above his head.

Something whirred past his ear and exploded in a shower of rock, spraying him with fragments of stone. *I'm gonna die now, I know I'm gonna die.* The thought was locked in his head on a loop. *I'm gonna die now, I know I'm gonna die.* The helter-skelter swerved sharply, flinging Ethan sideways round a bend. Not a moment too soon, as three more shots zipped past him, punching holes in the stone wall. Grit rained down upon his head as he tumbled over and over. *Phut, phut, phut.* The muffled shots spat from above him as his feet overtook his head and sent him into an uncontrollable spin. He twirled round and round, and just as he thought things couldn't get any worse, he suddenly became airborne. Arms and legs flailing, he flew through the darkness, somersaulting and twisting. Seasickness flooded through him as his stomach lurched and heaved. A pair of strong cold hands dug into his hair and yanked him sideways. 'Aaah help!' He wriggled and squirmed as an icy cold palm slapped across his face and clamped his mouth shut.

'Keep quiet, and for goodness' sake, stop bucking like a donkey. I think we've outrun him.' The familiar voice of Lake Splashdown hissed in his ear as he landed with a painful bomp. A thin grey light had broken the treacle-thick blackness, and Ethan could see they were in a cave about the size of his bedroom. Sharp spiky rock formations stuck out of the floor. A few centimetres to the left, and he would have been skewered. In the weak half-light he watched the incomplete shape of Lake Splashdown become solid once again. Shapeless pools of crystal-clear liquid became feet, legs and body. He straightened his hat and smoothed his moustache. 'The guards won't be far behind, so we'd better scram.'

'What was that thing?'

'That was the esteemed Doctor Freeze. He is Puddlemere's senior surgeon and scientist. He is a water elemental made entirely from ice. It's rumoured he caused Black Funday. That was the day all the enjoyment was sucked out of Puddlemere, and he blamed it all on your race.'

Ethan scrambled to his feet. 'Why would he do such a thing?'

Before Lake had a chance to answer, he started to shake uncontrollably. He pressed his hands to the side of his head. 'Oh no, not now, please.'

'What's wrong? What's happening?' Ethan watched as his companion jerked and jumped.

'Fun essence. It's pumped throughout Puddlemere. It makes us have fun, even if we don't want to. Ohhh, give me a break, pleeease.'

Ethan watched as Lake fought against it. Without warning, he back flipped and dropped down into the splits. Springing to his feet, he catapulted into the cave wall, exploding in a shower of water, tinkles of induced laughter permeating the small cavern.

'Lake, we've got to get out of here. I think I can hear the guards coming.'

'Don't you think I realise that?' said a hopping Lake. 'There's nothing I can do to stop this.' Lake spun around until he turned into a whirlpool, which in turn became an ornamental fountain. Ethan tried to grab him, but it was no use. It was like trying to hold on to smoke. The sprays of water shimmied in the pale light until Ethan yelled, 'Will you stop that!' The waterspouts dropped to the floor forming a blue-white puddle. In a few seconds it had reassembled itself into Lake Splashdown.

'Right, err.' Lake Splashdown seemed confused. He stared around the small cave, then at Ethan.

'We've gotta go. Come on.' Ethan grabbed Lake's shoulders and shook him hard.

'Go?' Lake's vacant expression slowly cleared. 'Go? Oh yeah, that's right.' The fog appeared to lift, and Lake shook his head. 'Well, what are you standing around for? the exit's that way.'

CHAPTER 7

The Dryads

Ethan squeezed through an impossibly small gap in the rock and popped out onto a narrow stony beach. Stumbling forwards, he overbalanced and landed face down with a splash. Coughing and spluttering, he spat out a mouthful of metallic tasting cave water.

'We'd better get back to the Dryads' hideout said Lake splashdown. We're too exposed out here on the ruby lake.' He dragged Ethan upright. 'Climb on, and I'll give you a piggyback.'

With a feeling of deja vu, Ethan clambered onto Lake's shoulders and held on tight. Within seconds, they were zipping through a dark network of underground canals and backwaters. Vast cliffs of grey rock closed in on both sides as Lake navigated the maze of waterways with expert ease. The sparkling emeralds, rubies and diamonds of the wide main areas of Puddlemere were nowhere to be seen. They passed long forgotten warehouses propped up on rotting poles, stumps of logs where piers used to be, and rusting cranes seized solid from disuse. The sharp tang of the main waterways had turned to a musty smell of rotten wood and old engine oil. On and on they travelled through the labyrinth of abandoned industry until they reached a derelict watermill. The old wooden building balanced dangerously across the narrow canal at an angle that made it look as if it was resting on one elbow. The left-hand-side had slumped, and it sagged down towards the water in the middle. This had made the tiles slide, which in turn had caved the roof in on one side.

'Here we are,' said Lake. 'Home sweet home.'

As they neared the abandoned mill, Ethan could see the remains of peeling white paint on wooden boards and an enormous rusty water wheel.

'You live here?' Ethan stared at the tired looking structure. A slate slid across the roof and disappeared through a yawning hole with a clatter.

'No. I've brought you here on a sightseeing tour. Follow me and stay close.'

Ethan watched as the elemental shimmied towards the rusty water wheel and squeezed through a gap where one of the paddles used to be.

Lake turned back to look at Ethan. 'Will you hurry up, for water's sake.'

Ethan swam along the murky canal eyeing the creaking building. 'Are you sure it's safe?'

'No, but what are you going to do, call the Puddlemere council? Just move it, will you!'

Batting an old tin can and a bit of door frame out of the way, Ethan swallowed his fear and heaved himself through the hole. Shafts of grey light filtered through from above. Where the wooden flooring used to be, a skeletal framework of worm-eaten beams criss-crossed above his head. A juddering groan came from the old mill, showering debris down into the water.

'Over here.' The voice came from behind one of the huge logs that just about propped up the near-collapsed building. 'This is where I need you to take a deep breath and stay close to me.' Lake dipped under the oily surface.

Ethan took a deep breath and dived. His water-logged clothes dragged him down into the murky green half-light. Ahead of him, Lake danced through the water with the grace and precision of a cat. Ethan kicked out clumsily, creating a cloud of silt that turned the water to soup. He was instantly lost. Not only could he not tell which way was forward or back, he wasn't entirely sure which way was up. Escaping dissection only to drown. Drown? He *was* going to drown unless he stopped panicking. A familiar face swam out of the murk, and a hand beckoned. Pulling hard, he swam downwards following Lake's vague outline. What little light there was, had now seeped away leaving Ethan in smothering wet blackness. But worse than that, the tunnel they were swimming through had suddenly narrowed. What if he got stuck? Lake Splashdown was made from water and could get through the smallest of spaces. He was one hundred percent solid. There was no way *he* could turn into water and seep through a tiny gap. His imagination showed him wedged in a rocky shaft inches from the surface and unable to move. With burning lungs desperate for air, he felt the tunnel widen and level out. He was sure he was going upwards again, and wasn't that a glimmer of light up ahead? With renewed hope he pulled against the weight of water. A dancing orange glow lit on the fragments of suspended debris. Flame light, he was sure of it. He'd nearly made it. All he had to do was hold on a few seconds more. He broke the surface with a heaving gasp. Oxygen. Sweet, sweet oxygen. He spluttered, spitting out a mouthful of brackish water as hands grabbed at him and heaved him onto dry land.

'Welcome to the Dryads' headquarters. It ain't the Ruby palace, but the rent's cheap,' said Lake.

Ethan collapsed onto his hands and knees, coughing and retching.

'Come on, up you get. It's time for the tour,' said Lake. Ethan was pulled upright. 'This way.' The short rock tunnel was lit by the flames of spitting reed torches. Black smoke drifted lazily upwards from the wall mounted lights and greased the air just above their heads. Rounding a bend in the passage, they stepped out into an enormous cave. A vast petrified waterfall of glimmering white covered the rear of the cavern. A round table, big enough to seat at least a hundred had been carved out of the living rock. Around this huge table were, who Ethan assumed to be, Dryad members, and they all sat on chairs carved from single gemstones. Their murmuring voices fell silent when Ethan stepped into view.

'Ladies and gentlemen,' said Lake. 'May I present to you, the Overlander. This is Myles Ethan Myles.' The roomful of water-people stared in Ethan's direction.

'So, it is true.' The voice came from an elderly elemental clothed in a flowing green cape embroidered with emeralds.

'Yes, Eldermaster Rain,' said Lake Splashdown. 'The emperor gave the go-ahead for Doctor Freeze to dissect Myles Ethan Myles.' Eldermaster Rain eased himself out of his chair and shuffled towards Lake and Ethan.

'What does he know?' Misty eyes peered out of a shrivelled, slightly shrunken face. Wispy white hair floated over the eldermaster's head giving the impression of a cloud that followed him wherever he went.

'Very little, and I propose we tell him everything, as this affects him and his entire race.' Lake led Ethan to an empty chair made from a single carved diamond.

Eldermaster Rain cleared his throat. 'We are the Dryads. We are a secret organisation opposed to Emperor Monsoon and the real power behind the throne, Doctor Freeze.' He spoke in a slow, measured tone and paused for half a beat before continuing. 'Many years ago, a huge explosion rocked Puddlemere, releasing potent gasses into the water. These gasses created a compound that sucked all of the enjoyment from our world. That terrible day became known as Black Funday. We have long suspected Doctor Freeze had a hand in the disaster, as he was forever working on more and more dangerous experiments.' Eldermaster Rain let out a rattling cough that shook his frail body. 'Forgive me, I've been overdosed with fun essence, and at my age it's not a good thing.'

Once Eldermaster Rain had composed himself, Ethan spoke up. 'Lake told me a bit about this stuff. What is it?'

Eldermaster Rain straightened up and smoothed his cape. 'Fun essence is the physical form that enjoyment takes. It resides within all humans and is especially potent in the young. Doctor Freeze devised a way of removing it, using an invention he calls the Fun Ultra Nebuliser. The more highly tuned the sense of fun is, the more potent the essence will be. This essence is then fed into the fun machine, which pumps it out into Puddlemere, giving all of us the pleasure missing from our lives.'

'So, Doctor Freeze has been stealing kids' fun?' Ethan could barely believe what he was hearing. But then again, if he'd been told about a race of people made from water only a few hours ago, would he have believed that?

'And it's one of the nicer things he does,' said Lake.

Eldermaster Rain held up a withered hand. 'The emperor believes everything Doctor Freeze tells him, and he's been fed lie after lie. The doctor told him that your people caused the explosion on purpose, giving him an excuse to steal your fun.' Eldermaster Rain coughed once again and dropped to one knee.

'Are you OK?' Ethan rushed to his side, but the eldermaster brushed him off.

'I'm fine. I just need a few seconds.' He eased himself back into his emerald chair and took a deep breath. 'Where was I? Oh yes, I remember. The Overlanders' fun has been seeping away for many years. That is the story Doctor Freeze has told the emperor. He claims that all of the unrest going on in your world is due to a lack of fun essence and is the reason why our fun was stolen from us.'

'So, to justify stealing human fun, Doctor Freeze made up a story about humans stealing Puddle peoples' fun. Is that right?' asked Ethan.

'Yes, but also to take the focus away from his dangerous experiments,' said the eldermaster. 'Our spies have informed me that you were due to have your brain removed by Doctor Freeze.'

Before the eldermaster could continue, Ethan leapt to his feet. 'That's right!' he shouted. 'The emperor said my brain was a recording device, and they needed to take it out so they could play back the information. That's insane!'

'Calm yourself. You're amongst friends now. No harm can come to you here.' Eldermaster Rain rested a hand on Ethan's arm. 'You are a very special boy. Your fun essence is highly developed, so I'm told.'

'Yeah,' said Ethan. 'That's what the emperor told me.'

'This is why they want the recipe. So they can reproduce it,' said Eldermaster Rain.

'Well, I don't feel like having any fun right now. In fact, I've felt miserable ever since I got an electric shock out in the garden.'

This time it was Eldermaster Rain who rose to his feet. 'You felt a jolt of electricity followed by a steady draining of happiness. You've felt irritable and angry ever since. That's right, isn't it?'

Ethan frowned. 'How do you..? The fun machine. It's stolen my essence, hasn't it?'

'I'm afraid so.'

'Excuse me, Eldermaster.'

Eldermaster Rain turned to face Lake Splashdown. 'He'll need to retrieve his essence before it's fed into the fun machine and lost forever,' said Lake.

'Yes indeed. If his essence is used, he will never regain his sense of fun. That would be an extremely dark day for him.'

'What about the weird glowing crystal I found in my garden?' said Ethan.

'What weird glowing crystal?' Lake asked.

'When I was searched, they took it and told me it was called rose quartz, or something, and accused me of stealing it. The emperor went off on me when he saw it.'

'This crystal,' said Lake. 'Was it pink with gold flecks?'

'Yes, and it did some really weird things,' said Ethan.

'Did it light up and hum?'

'Yes,' said Ethan.

Lake turned to face Eldermaster Rain. 'Rose gold quartz.'

The eldermaster nodded. 'Myles Ethan Myles,' he said. 'What you had in your possession was incredibly rare and powerful. It is called rose gold quartz, and it is a type of battery which never runs down. There are quite a few small ones, and by small I mean a millimetre or so long. How big was the one you had?'

Ethan thought for a brief moment. 'About ten centimetres long. It wasn't massive, or anything.' He shrugged.

'The missing fun machine crystal,' said Lake. 'I'm sure of it. There are only two crystals of that size in existence, and they are both used to power the fun machine. How did it end up in Overland?'

'Where are my manners?' The eldermaster rapped the table with his knuckles. 'Somebody fetch Myles Ethan Myles some refreshments and show him to the guest quarters. It is time for us to make plans.'

A cut crystal jug full of a clear pale blue liquid was placed in front of Ethan, along with a large two handled stoneware cup.

'Don't stand on ceremony,' said Lake. 'Drink up.'

A faint peppermint tang rose from the jug. 'What is this stuff'?' Ethan asked as he eyed the contents of his cup.

'Honestly, youngsters today. They don't know puddle draught from piddle.' Lake rolled his eyes. 'Trust me,' he said. 'It's good for you.'

'Puddle draught?' muttered Ethan, as he took a sip. His eyes went wide when the strange liquid hit his taste buds. Tipping his head back, he drained it in one go.

'Feel better now?' Lake asked.

Ethan burped loudly and nodded. 'This is so weird. It feels as if I've just eaten a massive dinner.'

'I told you it was good for you,' said Lake with a grin. 'Puddle draught is liquid food full of vitamins, minerals and marrowbone jelly.'

Ethan stared at Lake in disgust.

'I was joking about the marrowbone jelly.'

The sound of rushing water made Ethan turn his head towards the entrance tunnel. A spinning column of liquid burst into the meeting chamber. Within seconds it had re-materialised into the form of a young female Puddle person.

'Commander Splashdown, I have dire news.' The elemental girl looked a couple of years older than Ethan and wore a black and white waitresses uniform. Her bright green hair was pulled up into a tight bun, but a few strands had escaped and cork-screwed down to her cheek. 'A junior Overlander has fallen into Puddlemere and has been captured by the emperor.'

'That's old news, Brook. He's been rescued,' said Lake as he pointed to Ethan. 'Brook Backwater, meet Myles Ethan Myles.'

Brook gave Ethan a cursory glance. 'Permission to speak, sir,' said Brook.

'Go ahead.'

'Using the informants in the ruby palace, I have discovered the captive is female and goes by the name of Amber Myles.'

CHAPTER 8

The Rescue Mission

'That's my sister!' What was she doing in Puddlemere? If he hadn't insisted on showing her the puddle, she wouldn't have fallen in. He'd told her he wished she had never been born, and now she was going to be experimented on by that evil ice man. She was going to die, and it was all his fault. He knew he should have been kinder to her over the years. Like the time he put a frog in her lunch box, or when he let the tyres down on the bike she got for her eighth birthday. His stomach lurched at the thought, and his head felt light. Guilt and remorse were crushing him. What was he going to do? He jumped to his feet, knocking the heavy diamond chair to the ground. Acid bile rose in his throat, burning his gullet. He swallowed hard. 'We've got to save her!'

Eldermaster Rain rose slowly to his feet. 'Commander Splashdown, I do believe we have an emergency situation that needs to be dealt with speedily.' Discussions quickly turned to arguments as a hundred voices debated the best way of saving Amber. Storm the palace, said some, whilst others suggested meeting with the emperor. An undercover operation using Dryads disguised as delivery men was dismissed, as they had no uniforms. The babble of voices filled the room with a discord of noise.

'Quiet!' yelled Lake Splashdown. Silence was instantaneous. 'Thank you.' He climbed onto the table, and, looking around the room at the glistening wet faces, he began to speak. 'Do I have your undivided attention?' Everybody nodded, including Ethan. 'Good. I know the layout of the palace better than anyone here, as I was, as you know, a colonel in the imperial guard for many years. Taking it by force would be nothing short of suicide. As for trying to reason with the emperor, well, forget it. I shall go in alone. It's the best way.' Lake jumped to the floor and headed for the exit, when Ethan caught hold of his arm.

'I'm coming with you,' he said quietly. 'I know it's dangerous, but I don't care. She's my sister.'

Lake held Ethan with a steady gaze. 'I can't allow you to. If anything happened to you, I'd never forgive myself. Besides, I'd be quicker going alone. Anyway, I'll only be a few hours. Just you wait and see.' As Lake turned to leave, the air in the cavern crackled with energy. The hairs on Ethan's arms stood on end. It felt as though a rolling ball of thunder was about to be unleashed.

'Oh no, not again,' groaned Lake. 'Give me strength.'

Turning slowly towards Ethan, Lake grimaced. 'Fun essence.' Every Puddle person vibrated with barely controlled emotion, as the essence flooded through the chamber. The room had fallen silent, except for an undertone like humming electricity pylons. The air was thick with anticipation, as the elementals started to twitch and jerk. A titter escaped on the far side of the room, followed by a chuckle. Before Ethan knew what was happening, a full-scale party had erupted throughout the entire cavern. A band played near the petrified waterfall, whilst a group of people twisted and gyrated on top of the stone table. Ethan sunk to the floor and stared in disbelief. His sister had been kidnapped. How on earth could they party at a time like this? Lake Splashdown spun around on his head, as Eldermaster Rain moon-walked around him. A dozen or so played leapfrog and sang a tuneless sea shanty.

This had to stop. Urgent need pushed rational thought to the back of Ethan's mind. Getting Amber back eclipsed everything. Nothing else mattered. He jumped to his feet and grabbed Eldermaster Rain by his emerald cape. 'You have to stop this!' he yelled, as he tried to shake some sense into the old elemental. 'Amber's out there somewhere having who knows what done to her!'

The eldermaster stared vacantly at Ethan and continued his dance. Ethan pushed his way through the crowd and scrambled on to the huge round table. 'Will you lot stop this stupid party and help me?' he screamed, but nobody paid him any attention. Grabbing the two-handled cup, he hurled it at Lake Splashdown. A hand shot out and snatched it from the air. Ethan then flung the crystal jug. A second hand snaked up, plucking it from space. Glancing down at Lake, Ethan watched in frustration as the commander of the Dryads started juggling. This burst was much stronger than the earlier wave. Ethan jumped off the table. Yelling and throwing things hadn't worked. He stomped across the room, shoving dancers aside as he went.

It wasn't long before the party began winding down. Ethan had been to parties. He'd even had a few of his own, but he'd never seen them come to an end like this. People usually said goodbye, and then they left. They didn't drop to the floor as though switched off by an unseen hand. Puddle people were collapsing all around him. First in ones and twos, then six and seven at a time, until entire groups had their strings cut and folded to the floor like discarded marionettes. He looked around the cavern. Bodies lay sprawled across the floor, slumped over the table and draped over the gemstone chairs. After the noise of the party, the silence felt a little too quiet. A steady drip, drip, drip sounded in the stillness, as Ethan slowly made his way through the mass of unmoving elementals.

'Lake, where are you?' The only answer he received was his own echo. He had never felt so lonely as he did just then. He was in a room full of people but was, at the same time, utterly alone.

'This is useless,' he said to the unconscious crowd. 'I've got to work something out for myself before it's too late.' As he walked slowly through the cavern, his foot caught on something. Looking down to see what he'd nearly tripped over, he discovered the still shape of Lake Splashdown tucked behind a rock. 'Lake, wake up. It's Ethan.' He shook the commander as hard as he could but was greeted by a look of total emptiness. Lake's eyes were wide open and focused on nothing at all. There was no way Ethan could do this alone. He needed help. He needed Lake. 'Come on, wake up. You can't be in a coma. Not now. I need you to find my sister.' He slapped Lake hard around the face. 'Nothing. This is hopeless.' He let Lake flop to the ground. 'That's it then, it's over.' He let the tears flow as thoughts of never seeing his sister again filled his head.

'What's over?'

Ethan wasn't sure whether he'd imagined it or not, but he thought he heard Lake speaking. 'Is that you?' He wiped a sleeve across his face.

'Is what me?' Lake pushed himself up onto his elbows and looked around the Dryads' headquarters as if seeing it for the first time. 'Where am I? Who are you?' The brain fog was much worse this time.

'It's me, Ethan.'

Lake got slowly to his feet, holding on to the rock he'd been tucked behind. 'Ethan?' Lake screwed up his face. 'The name seems familiar, but I can't seem to place it.'

'Myles Ethan Myles,' said Ethan.

'Myles Ethan Myles. Yes, of course. It's coming back to me now. You fell into Puddlemere.'

'That's right. What else can you remember?'

'I, err, no, don't tell me.' Lake gripped his head in both hands. 'You fell into Puddlemere and, um.'

'Come on, Lake. Think harder. You can do it. You're the head of the Dryads. You're their leader.'

The congregation stirred all around them and a low murmuring had broken the church-like silence.

'I have to save your sister. Her name is Amber, and she's been captured.'

Ethan stood back and watched as Lake Splashdown's memory came back online.

'I thought you and everyone else had fallen into a coma,' said Ethan. 'I was sure I'd lost you for good. What did it do to you this time?'

'Well,' said Lake. 'We're never sure how strong each blast is going to be. Sometimes it only lasts a few seconds, but there are times when it can last a whole day. We have to dance and party for hours. The aftereffects are awful.'

'Yeah, I can see that. I thought you were off with the fairies for good.'

Lake gave Ethan a resigned look. 'When the machine pumps out the essence, we're at its mercy.'

With surprisingly renewed vigour, Lake shook off his subdued expression. 'I believe there is a damsel in distress awaiting rescue. I'll see you in a few hours, my friend.' Lake strode towards the passageway, turned the corner and was lost from sight.

Time dragged as Ethan waited impatiently for Lake to return with Amber. He'd been shown to the guest quarters but could not relax. The little room had been carved out of the solid rock and housed a bed made from thousands of precious gems. Ethan slumped down onto the water filled mattress and stared at the rocky ceiling for what felt like hours. Since breaking his phone, he had no idea of the time. He could have been waiting for minutes, hours, even days.

Lake said he'd only be a few hours. Had a few hours passed already? If so, how many hours *were* a few hours. Fond memories of Amber filled his head. Swinging his legs down onto the floor, he got up. He had to do something. This waiting around was just too much. Opening the door to his room, he peeped out. A crazy game of blind-man's buff was taking place at the far end of the cavern. It was another blast of fun essence. If Lake got a blast whilst rescuing Amber, anything could have happened to them.

Making his way down the smoke-filled corridor towards the exit hole, he peered into the water. The swim was not going to be easy, but he'd managed it before, so he could do it again. Taking as deep-a-breath as he could, he braced himself and jumped in. The cold greasy water filled his nostrils. He breathed in involuntarily, but instead of choking, he discovered he could breathe underwater. What was going on? This was impossible. He bobbed around in the green half-light trying to come to terms with the fact that he could breathe like a fish. He could also see clearly. Instead of the usual vague fuzziness he got when he swam without goggles, he had pin sharp vision. Small pieces of flotsam drifted by, and he could see every single detail, right down to the individual flecks of rust.

Kicking out, he propelled himself down into the gunge and through the maze of flooded tunnels. He was soon amongst the rusting hulks of machinery and abandoned industrial waste. Pushing up towards the skin of the water, he broke the surface. The cold grey light filtered down through the rotten planking above his head, picking out dancing specks of dust. The old mill juddered, sending a dozen or so roofing slates splashing down around him. Water breathing wouldn't save him from a cave-in and as he wriggled out through the gap in the water wheel, a plank broke free from behind him. It hit the water, flinging floating debris in all directions. It was just as well he got out when he did. If he'd dithered, the beam would have crushed him.

Now he was out in the open, he had time to think and to plan. Pulling himself up onto a deserted pier, he sat and pondered his situation. He could breathe and see underwater. He could also swim better than he'd ever been able to before. He sat down and considered his adventures so far. The only thing he'd eaten or drunk was puddle draught. 'Puddle draught, that's it,' he said aloud. 'It gives me some of the abilities of the Puddle people.' He still had a major problem, however. How was he going to sneak into the palace unnoticed? And even if he did manage to get in, where was he going to look first?

He set off in the general direction of the palace, swimming through the abandoned remains of the old industrial area. Broken windows and smashed doorways created sightless leering skulls with jagged fangs. The deep shadows of alleyways hid unseen creatures of the afterlife. He knew it was only his imagination, but he shuddered nonetheless and accelerated on through the maze of dead industry.

◆ ◆ ◆

He eventually arrived at the narrow stony beach he'd previously visited, following his earlier escape from Doctor Freeze. He needed to climb up the rocky shaft and back to the cell. If someone had left the door open, he would have access to the palace. Before he had a chance to lose his nerve, he squeezed through the narrow opening. Peering into the darkness, he could just make out the mouth of the chute he'd shot out of with Lake Splashdown.

Jumping as high as he could, he just managed to grip the bottom edge of the opening. It was smooth from centuries of running water, but he held on and hauled himself into the hole.

The tunnel was about the same size as the water chute at the local swimming pool and just as slippery. Climbing up a slide wasn't as easy as coming down it, but then again, secret rescue missions were *never* easy, were they?

After ten metres, the thin light seeping in from the mouth of the cave ceased entirely. He was as good as blind. So long as he kept going steadily upwards, he should, in theory, reach the cell.

The gentle slope stopped abruptly, jacking up to a near vertical shaft. To make matters worse, it led off in two different directions. He stared blindly into the new opening. There was no way he could remember which way he'd come. Well, he *was* being shot at the last time he was here. That kind of thing stops you from taking notes. Reaching a hand forwards, he felt a slight breeze coming from the right-hand passage. He sniffed the air. It Smelt like the cell. He eased into the right-hand entrance, hoping it was the correct one. Pushing his feet against one side of the shaft, and his back against the other, he began the slow walk upwards. One agonising step after another, he ascended the stone pipe until his foot touched something spongy. An instant feeling of weight-lessness filled him with dread. His feet had slid away from the tube, and he was about to take the express elevator all the way to the bottom.

'Oh no. No, no, no!' His head cracked against the tunnel wall, sending a burst of light across his vision. Sliding feet first back the way he came, he jammed his hands against the sides of the stone pipe. The water-slicked surface felt as though it had been greased. He pushed outwards with all of his might and gradually slowed to a stop. Pushing his feet out, he started his ascent once again. He'd burned through a lot of energy trying to stop his fall, and this time the climb was far harder. He knew he wouldn't get another chance, so he took his time. He mustn't slip. Not again. One tiny shuffle after another led him ever upwards. Every muscle in his body screamed for him to stop, but he knew he had to keep going. He counted. One, two, three. Every tiny step was a centimetre closer to his goal. Twenty-seven, twenty-eight, twenty-nine. He looked up. There it was, a ring of light cutting through the blanket of darkness. He was nearly there.

The chink of light came from the edge of the rock that fit the top of the shaft almost perfectly. Wedging himself hard against the tunnel walls, he reached up and pushed. The rock was incredibly heavy and took all of Ethan's strength and concentration to shift. It slid sideways with a nailson-blackboard grinding sound, before catching on something and sticking fast. With his fingers fumbling with the edge of the rock, he heaved. His legs now trembled and sweat stung his eyes. If he slipped, he'd end up at the bottom of the tube without the strength to climb back up. That wasn't an option.

He shoved as hard as he dare. The stone freed itself suddenly, giving Ethan nothing to hold on to. The muscles in his legs gave out, and his feet dropped from under him. Reaching desperately, he grabbed the top of the rock tube and gripped its rough edge. The uneven surface dug into his palms as he pulled with his last remaining reserves of energy.

lying on the familiar cell floor, his breath came in ragged gasps. He'd made it; this far, anyway. As his galloping pulse dropped out of the heart attack zone, he got gingerly to his feet and flexed his muscles. His legs shook wildly, and when he held out a hand, it quivered uncontrollably. His body was telling him to rest after the hard climb, but he had to press on; he didn't have any choice.

Creeping over to the cell door, he discovered that the guards had forgotten to lock it, and it was slightly ajar. He peeped through the small gap. He couldn't see anyone, but that didn't mean there was nobody there. He held his breath and listened for any movement in the corridor. Hearing nothing, he eased the door open. He'd got this far without being caught. That meant that the chances of capture were going steadily upwards. It had something to do with, what his maths teacher called, the law of averages. If you did something for long enough, there was more chance of it going wrong. With that non-comforting thought going around in his head, he stepped out into the passage. Looking left and right, he puffed out his held breath. He was alone. If the door slammed shut, though, the noise would bring the guards running, and he wouldn't be alone for long. Placing a small stone at the bottom of the door, he closed it to.

Should he turn left or right? If he turned right, he would pass the storerooms and kitchens. There was no laboratory that way. At least he didn't think so. With no other available choice, he turned left. The corridor corkscrewed steadily downwards, and he inched along, stopping at the slightest sound. Click. That's when he heard it. It was a nearby door being shut.

CHAPTER 9

Fire and Ice

'That Doctor Freeze gives me the creeps.' The voice drifted up the corridor from just ahead of him.

'Keep it down, Drizzle, for water's sake. If he hears you, he'll use you for one of his experiments.'

Ethan's mouth went dry. He couldn't have more than a few seconds before the guards rounded the bend. Turning around, he ran as quietly as he could. That was the moment his maths teacher's theory proved to be correct. His foot clipped a stone and sent it skittering across the floor. The pebble must have been tiny, and in normal circumstances he wouldn't have even noticed it. Now his and Amber's lives depended on him not being heard, however, it clattered and echoed as it bounced and pinged down the stone passageway.

'Here, Drip. Did you hear that?'

Ethan froze. He'd been discovered, and there was nowhere to hide. He looked around, frantically searching for an escape route.

'Hear what?'

'I'm not sure. Let's check it out.'

The sound of footsteps echoed in the dingy corridor. Unless Ethan did something immediately, he was going to get caught. But what *could* he do? The storerooms and kitchens were too far. They'd catch him before he got anywhere near them. The footsteps were getting steadily closer. In less than five seconds, the guards would round the curve in the corridor, and then it wouldn't matter what he did. He had to move, and it had to be now. The rush of adrenaline caused his wobbly legs to tingle as he fled up the corridor, heedless of any noise he was making. He had to think of something. He had to think of... That's when it came to him. The cell! He had to get back to the cell. If he hid in there, they might run past the door, allowing him to double back behind them.

'I can hear them, Drip. They're getting away.'

'They can't get far. We'll have them in no time.'

The sound of boots echoed around the walls. Ethan sprinted hard and skidded to a halt as he reached the cell door. He shoved it open and pushed it shut against the little stone.

'Shh! Let me listen,' said Drip from outside the cell door. 'The footsteps have stopped, so they must be here somewhere.'

What was he thinking? Like an idiot, he'd got himself trapped. He should have kept going. At least he'd have had the chance to outrun them. Now he'd gone and locked himself in the prison they had put him in originally. If they came into the cell now... Ethan shook his head. No, not if. When.

'The cell door. It's open,' said Drizzle.

That was it, he was finished. They were right outside and were coming in. He didn't stand a chance. His adrenaline drained away in the face of resignation, leaving him weak and trembling with fatigue. He stared hopelessly at the hole waiting for the door to open. That's when his mind did one of those curious A to B via X things. The hole was going to save his life and hopefully Amber's as well.

'Well, of course it's open. It's never locked when it's unoccupied. There's no point,' said Drip.

Hoping Drizzle and Drip would keep up their constant stream of babble, Ethan crept over to the hole in the floor and pulled over the cover.

'I know it's never locked when it's unoccupied,' said Drizzle. 'That's my point.'

Ethan eased himself down into the shaft and pulled the manhole cover over, until it fitted snugly into its hole. He didn't think his legs would hold him up, but what choice did he have? He could either wait to be captured, followed by brain removal surgery, or wedge himself at the top of the shaft with exhausted limbs, hoping that the guards wouldn't find him.

The door swung open and boots pounded the floor above. Holding his breath, he stared upwards at the crack of light circling the lid.

'Can you see anything back there?' A shadow fell across the bright ring as Drip stepped onto the manhole cover. Grit sifted down into Ethan's face, making his eyes smart.

'It's all clear,' said Drizzle. 'I think it's a false alarm.'

Unable to hold his breath any longer, Ethan breathed deeply, sucking in a lungful of dust.

'There's something in this cell that irritates my sinuses,' said Drizzle.

An explosive sneeze erupted from above, just as Ethan let out an uncontrollable cough.

'Did you hear something?' said Drip.

'Yeah,' said Drizzle. 'My nose explosion,' and he sneezed again.

'Seriously,' said Drip, 'I could have sworn I heard someone coughing.'

Ethan's legs shuddered violently, and cramp pains turned his muscles to burning rods of steel.

'There's nobody here, so let's go, OK?' Drizzle sniffed.

Ethan stared upwards. Why weren't they leaving? They were standing in an empty room, so why hang about?

'What about the drainage shaft?' Ethan's pulse increased. He was inside the drainage shaft. If they removed the lid, they would see him staring up at them, just before he disappeared down it. The ring of light returned as Drip stepped off the cover.

'There's no way anyone can lift this lid when it's wedged in properly,' said Drizzle. 'We've got to report to the sarge anyway. If we're late again, there'll be hell to pay.'

'Good point,' said Drip.

The door ground open, and the voices of Drip and Drizzle receded up the corridor. Deciding he couldn't wait a second longer, Ethan shoved the stone cover as hard as he could. It slid open with a loud clatter, but by this time he was in too much pain to care. Seizing the rough edge, he pulled himself up onto the uneven cave floor. The sharp rutted surface dug into his back, but he couldn't feel it over the pain in his legs. Rolling carefully onto his front, he struggled to his feet. The cramp had subsided, but his legs felt weak. If he had to run, he wouldn't get very far.

Drip and Drizzle had left the cell door wide open, giving Ethan a full view of the corridor beyond. He listened for approaching footsteps. Hearing none, he scanned the passage one last time before creeping out into the open. There was nobody there. If there was, what was the worst that could happen, anyway? Have his brain cut out by a lunatic doctor?

The dank passage was too wide, too long and too echoey. After his previous exploit he didn't want to be out here at all. But Amber was somewhere in the palace, and that meant he had a job to do. He'd gone downwards before, so should he risk going up into the palace proper? Or should he delve into the palace's underbelly? A friend had told him a joke last week. "I used to be undecided, but now I'm not so sure." He smiled ironically to himself and shook his head. That was when a small sign caught his attention. He was sure it wasn't there earlier. It may have been, but in all the excitement, he could have missed it. It was small; only about six centimetres long and the dull green of copper that's been left in the rain for too long. Engraved on its surface in capital letters was the word LABORATORY, and underneath was an etched arrow. The arrow pointed down the passage. 'Oh well,' he muttered to himself. 'Down it is, then.'

His ears strained for the slightest noise as he crept towards the lab. That must be where Amber was being experimented on. She was probably having the top of her head cut off at this very moment. The thought made him want to run down the passage, but he fought to restrain himself. If he sprinted, he wouldn't hear it if anyone came up towards him, but they'd hear him all right. He'd made it this far. He mustn't blow it. Breathing deeply to steady his fizzing nerves, he continued slowly downwards. After what felt like an hour but must have only been about five minutes, the corridor dead-ended at a frosted glass door. "Dr Freeze. Laboratory. No Unauthorised Entry." The raised letters cast small shadows across the door's pale surface. This was it. He'd arrived. Now what?

He glanced back over his shoulder to make sure nobody was behind him, then he looked down at the door handle. It was sleek and highly polished. His distorted reflection looked back at him, and he didn't like what he saw. A grubby urchin that he didn't recognise stared up with an expression of undiluted terror. That's when a small voice at the back of his mind told him to run. Run and never look back.

No. He mustn't give in to that cowardly whisper. His sister was in there. His sister that he'd said vile things to. She was going to die thinking he hated her, and all he could think about was running away. No, that wasn't going to happen. He was here to save her.

He gripped the handle in a trembling fist and turned. Nothing happened. He puffed out an almost relieved breath. The door was locked. Of course it was. Did he really think it was going to be that easy?

A single bead of sweat popped on his forehead and cut a ticklish track down his nose. It was cold in here, much colder than the cell, so why was he sweating? He drew a sleeve across his face. He had to stop wasting time and figure out how to get in. He studied the door and the handle but could find no lock and was on the verge of giving up when he spotted a chrome keypad with black buttons. A-Z and 0-9. It couldn't be something easy like 1-4, could it? He knelt down to get a better look at the buttons and on closer inspection, found three to be badly worn. O, H and 2. A man made out of water used the code H_2O, the chemical symbol for water as his entry code. Seriously? He peered at the frosted glass hoping for a clue as to where Doctor Freeze was. Nothing. He reached out a hand. All he had to do was press H_2O and he'd be in. His hand froze millimetres from the buttons. He was about to see that creature again. That creature that wanted him dead. His heart jack-hammered against his ribs and his breath came in short, ragged gasps. The urchin with the big, frightened eyes stared back at him from the shiny keypad, and the small voice at the back of his mind became a shout. "Run!" 'No,' he whispered defiantly and punched in H_2O. A red light blinked briefly on the keypad and Ethan slumped against the wall. His reserves of courage were running dangerously low. The code hadn't worked. Before his courage deserted him completely, he tried again. Still nothing.

The high-pitched whining of a dentist's drill came from the far side of the door. It was too late. He'd lost too much time. His vision blurred as fat salty tears splattered on the rough stone floor.

'Testing one, two, three.'

That was Doctor Freeze. He'd know that soulless voice anywhere.

'Preparations for brain removal nearly complete. Recording system check.'

Doctor Freeze hadn't started the operation yet.

That meant he still had the chance to save Amber. He ground his fists into his eyes to clear the tears and knelt by the keypad once more. If H_2O hadn't worked, that left O2H, 2OH, 2HO and OH2. Which one was it? Too many combinations. He punched in O2H and crossed his fingers and with a click, a green light flashed on. He'd done it. He'd cracked the code, but now he had to actually open the door and enter the lab. He grabbed the handle before urchin boy could talk him out of it, but the voice still spoke to him. "Get away while you still can." Every nerve in his body hummed like a high voltage cable, his head both light with dizziness and pounding with the rush of blood. He took a deep breath, turned the handle and silently slid the door open. If it was game over, there wouldn't be a re-try. He stepped into the laboratory.

There were bubbling test tubes, heated by Bunsen burners atop polished wooden workbenches. Shiny brass machines with cogs and pistons whirred and chuffed. An enormous steam engine sat at the end of the lab. Instead of wheels, it had cogs connecting to chains and pulleys which drove rods running the entire length of the ceiling.

Ducking down behind the first workbench, Ethan looked out across the room. One wall was partly taken up by handyman's tools. What really caught his attention, however, was a large stainless-steel trolley full of surgical instruments. Clamped onto a nearby operating table wearing glass shackles was his sister. He could feel the adrenaline singing in his system as Doctor Freeze leaned over her. Ethan's hands trembled as his fight-or-flight response went into high gear. He could neither fight nor flee, so what *was* he going to do? Indecision stung him hard as tears of frustration pricked at the corners of his eyes. Even though he knew it wasn't his fault, the guilt he felt for his harsh words burned fiercely. He didn't wish Amber had never been born. He knew that. He knew it even while he was saying it. What he didn't know though, was why Lake hadn't managed to rescue her.

'It's such a shame that you won't be able to witness your own dissection.' The icy cold voice of the doctor echoed in the sterile surroundings. 'Still, never mind.' The doctor moved away from Amber to peruse the trolley.

This might be his only chance. With the doctor's back to him, he could nip across the room to a glass fronted cabinet that stood close to the operating table. From there he could figure out what to do next. His heart raced and sweat slicked his palms. He had to go now, so why didn't he? He knew the risks, that's why. Dissection at the hands of a frozen lunatic. But he also knew what was *at* risk. His little sister, who he'd hurt with that stupid awful remark. If he didn't go now, he never would.

Crouching as low as he could, he scuttled crablike across the lab, not taking his eyes from the iceman for a second. If the mad doctor turned around now... He just didn't want to think about it. Sliding in behind the cabinet, he slowly released his breath.

'Now, young lady.'

Ethan peeked out from his hiding place. Doctor Freeze was discussing the dissection with Amber and was busy selecting different drill bits from the trolley.

'I'm going to start by drilling a small hole in your forehead. It will hurt, by the way.'

He knew that if he thought too hard, he'd never rescue her. He had to stop thinking and start doing and slipped from the cover of the cabinet. There was no going back now. He was in the open with nowhere to hide. Feeling like the only pea on an otherwise empty plate, he crept across to the operating table. 'Amber, it's me,' he whispered. 'Listen, I'm really sorry about what I said earlier, OK?' He removed her gag.

'Whatever,' she said in a low voice. 'Just get me out of here.'

Ethan examined the shackles. They were as clear as glass and as cold as ice.

'They're elemental shackles,' whispered Amber. 'They're made of ice. He told me they were as strong as steel; totally unbreakable.'

'They're made from ice?' Ethan was amazed. 'Ice can be melted. If I can heat a screwdriver over one of those Bunsen burners, I can free you in seconds.' He glanced up to check on Doctor Freeze, and his stomach dropped. Doctor Freeze was nowhere to be seen.

Ethan stared around the room. Where was the doctor? His skin prickled as the temperature suddenly dropped. A flash of bright metal flew across the room, and Ethan jerked sideways as his sleeve was pinned to the cabinet by a scalpel.

'Hello, boy.' Doctor Freeze stepped out from behind a metal filing cabinet, his eyes flashing a deep crimson. 'Easy to break in here, wasn't it? Did you follow the sign I left for you in the corridor?'

Ethan turned to flee. The bottles and jars in the cabinet jangled, as his sleeve tugged against the scalpel's blade.

'I thought a combination of H_2O would be simple for you to decipher. I couldn't just leave the door unlocked, could I? You would have been suspicious.'

Realisation dawned. Amber was bait. He'd been trapped.

'Ethan, run!'

Doctor Freeze turned to face Amber. Fabric tore as Ethan tugged at his sleeve. He stumbled forwards into the medical cart. Saws, drills and forceps scattered, as the wheeled trolley spun across the shiny white floor.

'What the..?' the smooth cold voice of Doctor Freeze roared in jagged spiky rage.

Ethan fell forwards and slid across the floor behind a workbench.

'Your sister falling into Puddlemere was fortuitous.' Doctor Freeze seemed to have got his temper under control. 'I knew you wouldn't be able to resist trying to rescue her.'

Ethan scanned the room from his hiding place. Doctor Freeze was walking slowly from bench to bench. It was only a matter of time before he was caught. Stuffing his hand into his pocket, he pulled out a two pence piece. He threw it as hard as he could across the lab. It pinged off the steam engine and clattered into the depths of the machinery. Deep-frozen footsteps hurried noisily. The doctor had fallen for his ruse. He was heading for the back of the lab.

Ethan knew he only had one chance, so he had to make it count. The bench he'd been hiding under was packed with all manner of scientific equipment. A round-bellied jar sat above the blue flame of a Bunsen burner. Dark green goop bubbled sluggishly, filling the air with a rotting-dog-food stench. Blop. A huge bubble burst, releasing a fresh wave of foul smells. Ethan held his breath and rifled through the various tools scattered across the work surface. An oversized soldering iron rested in a coiled spring. It was just the thing to melt Amber's shackles. He flipped the on-switch and pocketed some wire cutters, a screwdriver and a pair of electronics pliers just in case they came in handy.

'You've no idea how important your essence is.' The doctor's voice came from the far side of the massive steam engine and was getting nearer. 'It's the finest I've ever seen. Once I disassemble your brain, I can extract the recipe and formulate my own.'

Ethan hopped urgently from foot to foot. Why was the soldering iron taking so long to heat up? A gentle warmth had started to emanate from the wide flat blade, just as Doctor Freeze came back into view. Ducking behind the bench once more, Ethan knew he wouldn't be able to pull off the same stunt with the coin again. The slow and steady click, click, click of frozen footsteps drew nearer by the second.

Why hadn't he heated up a screwdriver in the Bunsen burner, like he'd planned? It would have been over by now.

Edging around to the far side of the bench, he reached up blindly for the iron. Searing agony shot through his hand, followed by the acrid smell of burning flesh. He bit down hard on his lower lip to stop himself from crying out. The soldering iron had heated up all right, but he'd grabbed the wrong end.

The clicking of icy feet stopped. Ethan risked a look and peered over the top of the work-bench. Doctor Freeze had stopped moving and was sniffing the air, like a cat sensing a mouse.

Reaching forward as carefully as he could, Ethan unplugged the hot iron, and lifted it from its cradle. The tip now glowed a dull red as if it had been left in a fire for too long. No wonder it hurt.

The footsteps resumed their relentless rhythm. Click: Closer. Click: Colder. A thin layer of frost was beginning to form as the evil ice man neared his prey. Tiny glittering crystals sparked in the harsh white light. The footsteps ceased. Doctor Freeze sniffed the air before continuing his slow walk.

He can smell my burnt hand, thought Ethan in alarm. He had to disguise the odour somehow, and fast. Bracing himself for discovery, he reached up and tipped the round-bellied jar on its side. A slow glub, glub, was followed by a bubbling hiss, as the goop hit the work surface. A nauseating stench of rotting meat filled the air.

'Oh, that *is* clever.'

Ethan couldn't be sure if the doctor was talking to him, or to himself.

'Full of fun *and* intelligence. You'll make a fine specimen.'

Gripping the correct end of the soldering iron, Ethan inched around the bench, away from Doctor Freeze, his breath clouding white in the rapidly cooling air. Peering around the corner of the workstation, he could see the mutant killer ice cube. He was less than a metre away but facing in the other direction.

Ethan took a deep breath, held it and slipped out from the cover of the bench. He watched Doctor Freeze in fascinated horror. The foul creature had resumed his sniffing. Ethan rammed his injured hand into his pocket to stop the doctor from tracking his scent. He sucked air through his teeth, as pain speared the burn. Doctor Freeze was statue-still.

He tried not to move, not to breathe and not to blink. The ice man had heard him, he was sure of it. Any second now that monster would turn around and lock onto his prey with those dead eyes of his. Time seemed to stretch as the doctor looked slowly from left to right. Seconds lengthened into minutes as Ethan crouched on juddering legs. *Please don't turn around.* As if in response to Ethan's unspoken request, Doctor Freeze shook his head and walked slowly towards the far end of the lab. Wasting no time, Ethan crept as quickly and as quietly as he could over to the glass fronted cabinet near the operating table.

'It's me,' he whispered and melted a hand shackle with the soldering iron. 'Take the iron,' he said to Amber, breathlessly. 'I'm going to keep him occupied, while you escape. I'll see you behind the bench by the door, in a minute.' He ran across the lab, keeping his head below the workstations. An intricate array of glass test tubes, bubbling with a pale pink liquid gave him an idea. Seizing a small saw from a bench top, he hurled it boomerang style at the apparatus, hoping it would divert Freeze's attention from Amber.

A loud bang erupted, and flying glass shot through the air. Doctor Freeze dived for cover, his hands over his face like a shield.

Ethan slipped out of sight behind a partition wall. It was quiet in the lab. Too quiet. The only sound was the lazy chuff of the steam engine and the occasional tinkle of glass as a piece of broken test tube rolled onto the floor. Where was Doctor Freeze? And why wasn't he screaming and shouting? A cold metal barrel pressed against his temple. That was why.

'I don't usually kill my prisoners before I experiment on them, but I'm willing to make an exception with you.'

Out of the corner of his eye, Ethan could make out a bulbous copper pistol, the same type the guards were armed with.

'Admiring my invention, are you? Its full name is a Hyperthermium pistol, or therm gun, for short.'

The chilling proximity of the doctor froze the sweat on Ethan's face.

'Hyperthermium 410 is a liquid that never freezes. It's always at a temperature just below absolute zero. If I were to shoot you, you would freeze solid in an instant.'

Ethan raised his hands in surrender.

CHAPTER 10

A Dangerous Substance

'Lab. Rats. Do. Not. Smash. Up. The. Lab.' With every exaggerated word, Doctor Freeze rapped Ethan on the head with the therm gun. 'Now get over there by the operating table.'

Ethan stumbled forwards as the doctor shoved him hard in the back.

'It's time to join your sibling. She can watch as I...' Doctor Freeze spun Ethan round and grabbed him by the throat. 'Where is she?' The doctor's eyes flashed bright red, before fading to black. 'Oh, I see what you've done. Clever brother, clever sister. Not clever enough, though.'

Over the doctor's shoulder, Ethan watched Amber creep out from behind the chemical cabinet, wielding a metal crutch.

The doctor's head snapped around. Too late.

Stainless steel flashed in the hard-white light and connected with a resounding clang. Shards of ice sparked as they sprayed high into the air. The doctor turned back to face Ethan, his eyes turning a milky white. The frozen hand released its icy grip from Ethan's throat, and the doctor fell backwards through the glass cabinet, tipping over a large glass jar. Clear liquid glugged from the jar's neck as it rolled to a stop. The rapidly spreading puddle hissed and smoked as it ate into the polished white flooring.

'Watch out, I think that's acid!' said Ethan. 'Let's go before he wakes up.'

Crunching across the broken glass, Amber stopped. 'Shh! I can hear someone coming.'

Voices drifted in through the frosted glass door. 'Why is it always us? I don't know about you, Drip, but I'll either puke or faint.'

'Not those two again.' Ethan took Amber's hand and pulled her around behind the partition wall. A large grey metal cabinet stood off to one side. Ethan turned the shiny chrome handle hoping it wasn't locked. The cool smooth lever twisted in Ethan's grip, then stuck fast.

'What in Puddlemere's happened here?' yelled Private Drizzle.

'I don't know, but keep the noise down. I think I heard something,' whispered Private Drip.

'Hurry up,' said Amber. 'They're in the room.'

Ethan jiggled the handle hoping it would free itself. 'I'm going as fast as I can,' he whispered.

'The noise is coming from over there. Drizzle, you go left, and I'll swing round to the right.'

Footsteps crunched nearer and nearer as Ethan frantically tried to open the cabinet. Struggling with the lever, he heard the crash of something metal hitting a hard floor, from the other side of the wall.

'Sorry, Drip,' came the voice of Private Drizzle. 'I've had a bit of an accident.'

The cabinet lever finally gave and opened with a loud clunk. Luckily, the noise coincided with another crash.

'It's only me again,' said Drizzle.

Ethan saw the clear watery feet of Private Drip come into view just before he closed the door behind him. Footsteps stopped outside the cupboard. Ethan gripped Amber's hand as the latch started to move. The mechanism turned in the darkness of the closed cabinet. Click, click, clunk. Light streamed in through the widening gap as the door swung open.

'Drip!' yelled Private Drizzle. 'You've got to see this!'

'Not now, I'm busy.' Drip turned towards the open cupboard once again.

Ethan's extraordinary run of luck had just run out. He'd been rescued from prison, escaped drowning and dissection but now none of that mattered. In less than half a second, they would be captured, and Drip would earn himself a medal. Ethan's mouth was dry, his palms were wet, and to his left, he felt Amber tremble. She knew they were both about to die. He could almost feel her thoughts. The worst thing about it was not being able to do anything. His job was to look after her, and he'd failed. Regret and remorse bit hard enough for him to almost feel physical pain. This was all because of that stupid puddle, and his insistence on showing it to her.

'Seriously, you have to see this.' Private Drizzle's urgent tone went up a notch. Drip turned in the direction of Drizzle's voice.

'What's so important?'

Hope had returned but hope was fickle. Ethan knew this. All it would take was for Drip to turn his head.

'It's Doctor Freeze!' Drizzle was shouting now. 'I think he's dead!'

Drip let go of the cupboard's handle, turned on the spot and raced around the partition wall towards Drizzle.

How long this seam of fortune would last, Ethan had no idea. But for the time being, at least, he was in the clear. He let out a breath he hadn't realised he'd been holding and inched out of the cupboard, leading Amber by the hand. Peering around the wall, Ethan could see both soldiers leaning over Doctor Freeze.

'He's dead, I tell you.' Drizzle was bent over the unmoving body and was prodding him with the stainless-steel crutch.

'I wouldn't be doing that, if I was you,' said Drip

as he backed away from the crumpled icy shape. 'What if he's not dead?'

From their hiding place, the kids watched Drizzle drop the metal crutch. It hit the floor with a clatter.

'Well, if he's not dead, I'm not sticking around waiting for him to wake up,' said Drizzle.

'Me neither,' said Drip. 'But we've got to report this to Sergeant Floodwater, so I vote we go and tell him. He's interrogating Lake Splashdown. Come on, let's hustle before the doctor wakes up.'

Ethan spoke quietly to Amber. 'If we follow these two, we'll be able to rescue Lake Splashdown. He's on our side. He's probably our only hope of escape.' Every sound seemed amplified as the kids tiptoed across the wrecked lab. Crunching glass sounded under their feet, as they made their way to the exit. The vague shapes of Drip and Drizzle were visible through the frosted glass door.

'I hope we don't get sent back to the lab,' said Drizzle.

'You and me both.'

'They've gone.' Ethan breathed a sigh of relief. 'Wait a few seconds, then we'll follow. We don't want to be too close.'

The corridor was extra gloomy after the bright white light of Doctor Freeze's lab. Ethan squinted in the semi-darkness as he edged forwards along the dimly lit passageway.

'We won't get in trouble for leaving Doctor Freeze, will we?' The voice of Private Drizzle echoed down the hallway. 'I'm going back to check on him. See if he's alive, or not.'

Amber gripped Ethan's hand as the wavering shadow of Private Drizzle grew larger and longer. Ethan needed a plan, but fear had fogged the workings of his mind. He took a step backwards, dragging Amber down towards the lab. He didn't have the first idea of what to do, except run. Every muscle in his body thrummed with nervous energy as the steady beat of Drizzle's boots got closer.

'Don't be so stupid,' said Drip. 'If yours is the first face Doctor Freeze sees if he wakes up, think what he'll do to you.'

The footsteps slowed to a stop.

'Good point,' said Drizzle.

The shadow retreated as Private Drizzle made his way back up the corridor.

Ethan looked at Amber. She was shaking her head. He didn't believe that had just happened, either. He took a deep breath and tried to slow his galloping pulse. They had to follow Drizzle and Drip if they wanted any chance of escape. So as tempting as it was just to let them go, he knew he couldn't. He looked Amber in the eye and pointed up the passageway. She nodded. He knew she'd follow him, but even so, he could feel the fear coming off her in waves. She was no less terrified than he was, but that wasn't the point. He was older than her. He had to be the grown up and lead the way. He just hoped it was the right decision. The two guards kept up a steady stream of babble, which made following them fairly easy. Ethan recognised this part of the corridor. They were nearing the cell. He motioned for Amber to stop. The guards had fallen silent, and that could only mean one thing. They had reached their destination, and Ethan had a pretty good idea what that destination was.

He crouched as low as he could and eased around the curve. He hadn't heard the cell door open. What if they were waiting for him? He dropped to the floor and crawled the last few feet. The corridor was empty. The coast was clear. He crept back to where Amber was waiting. 'Follow me,' he whispered.

'I've no need to explain to you the effects of hyperthermium, have I, Splashdown?'

The voice coming from the other side of the door was instantly recognisable to Ethan. It was that weasel, Storm Floodwater.

'I know about the soft spot you have for Overlanders. We've got a female on the operating table, right now,' said Storm. 'If you tell me where the Dryads' headquarters are, I will consider asking the emperor to let her go.'

Drizzle and Drip hadn't delivered their message. As he tried to figure out what to do next, his thoughts were interrupted as Amber prodded him in the arm. 'What?' he mouthed silently.

'The door is open,' mimed Amber.

Flickering torchlight cast dancing shadows on the wall behind them. 'I'm going to look.' Ethan silently pointed to his eyes, then at the door and easing forwards as quietly as he could, he peeked through the gap.

'You didn't rise through the ranks quite as quickly as you thought, did you?' said Lake. 'You were pathetic when I was your commanding officer but look at you now. You've risen all the way to colonel. No, wait a minute. That was me. You were a sergeant then, and you still are.' Lake Splashdown was shackled to an emerald chair. He stared up at Storm Floodwater with a look of contempt.

'At least I'm not a loser like your twin brother.' Storm sneered at Lake.

Lake's head dropped to his chest and in a barely audible voice, said, 'Don't you dare mention my brother. River was more of a soldier than you'll ever be.'

Through the narrow gap in the door, Ethan could see Drizzle and Drip standing with their backs to him. Next to the two privates was Storm Floodwater, who leaned over Lake. Held in his watery hands was a device that reminded Ethan of his dad's jet wash. A thin white mist puffed from the nozzle, falling lazily to earth. A coiled hose led from the jet wash gun to a round metal vat that was encrusted with ice. Ghostly vapour bubbled from the vat and poured over the side, filling the room with a blanket of ankle-deep horror film fog.

'Your brother...' said Storm.

'My brother,' cut in Lake, 'died collecting ghost glass from Porlock's Dread for that maniac, Doctor Freeze.' His voice rose steadily in volume.

'And whose fault is that?' Storm prodded Lake with the tip of his gun.

'He was under orders. When was the last time you defied the doctor?' Lake pulled on his shackles. 'He travelled the grey roads, you coward!' He screamed at Storm. 'Nobody's ever come back alive from there!'

'Whatever.' Storm waved a hand dismissively. 'Let's get back to the point of the conversation, shall we?' Poking Lake with the cannon once again, Storm continued. 'We have the female. She's in Doctor Freeze's lab at this very moment. I know you came here to rescue her, but thanks to a targeted blast of fun essence, you got caught. If you tell me where you and your band of traitors are hiding, I'll see if she can be released.'

'Err, sergeant.' Private Drip snapped to attention and saluted.

'What is it, Drip? Can't you see I'm busy.'

'I wouldn't normally interrupt an interrogation, but this is important, sarge.'

'OK, Drip. Out with it.'

'Well, err, it goes like this. The girl has escaped, and we think Doctor Freeze may be dead.'

Storm turned to face Lake. 'Is this true? Has your mob of rebels invaded the palace?' Storm Floodwater released the catch on the cannon and started to pump a wooden handle. The gun started to hiss, as the pressure slowly rose. The lazy mist wafting from the nozzle became a thin jet stream. 'You will tell me everything,' demanded Storm, as he pointed the weapon at Lake's left leg.

Ethan knew that if he just crept away now, he still had a chance of getting out of Puddlemere alive, but Lake had saved his life and was being tortured because he got caught trying to save Amber. No, he had to do something. He couldn't just slink away, like a coward.

'Tell me!' yelled Storm.

Ethan's damp clothing suddenly felt very heavy, and he shivered with cold feverish terror. What he was about to do was probably. No, definitely the stupidest thing he'd ever done in his life. Three armed elementals against him and his nine-year-old sister? He didn't have a hope. Or a plan. The only thing he did have was the element of surprise. Once he'd played that card, what then? He glanced at Amber. She frowned at him. She knew he was about to do something monumentally idiotic, but what else could he do?

He backed up as far as he could, until he felt rough stone against his back. His senses had heightened to a point where he swore he could almost hear light. Blood swished in his veins as his heart pumped like an express locomotive and every tiny drip whipcracked through his head. He focused hard on the door. On the other side were several possible outcomes, none of them good. Except for one tiny spark of a chance. It was lottery winning odds. He knew this, but one in several million was better than nothing at all, right? Before he could talk himself out of it, he pushed off from the wall, slammed through the door and ran screaming into the room.

He raced over to the vat and kicked it as hard as he could. Icy jets erupted from the cannon, like cold flames, as he dived for cover behind Lake's chair.

Private Drizzle drew his pistol and pointed it at Ethan. 'Stop right there, or I'll shoot!'

Realising the hopelessness of the situation, Ethan did as he was told.

'Oh joy,' said Storm. 'Maybe I will get that promotion, after all. Drip, inform his majesty that I have just captured the male escapee.'

Just as Drip turned to leave, a huge creaking groan came from the vat. One of the three metal legs it stood on folded inwards, and the canister lurched drunkenly to one side, sloshing its lethal contents over the edge. A wave of sub-zero fluid washed over Private Drip, freezing him instantly. The curly hose connecting to the cannon pulled tight, yanking it from Storm's grip.

'What have you done?' screeched Storm, as he lunged for the gun. The freezing metal container hit the stony floor with a loud clang, spilling its remaining contents. Storm looked up horrified, his right arm frozen up to the shoulder, hand gripping the now useless weapon. 'Drizzle, shoot him!' he yelled, but Private Drizzle didn't reply.

'Amber, give us a hand, will you?' called Ethan.

Amber stepped into the room, dodging around the frozen Private Drizzle. She hopped across the spreading pool of hyperthermium to where Ethan tugged at Lake's restraints.

'You need the key. It's on the bunch hanging from Storm's belt.' Lake nodded towards the immobilised sergeant. 'Whatever you do, though, don't touch the hyperthermium.' The smoking pool of fluid had solidified both of Storm's legs and his right arm and was spreading with every passing second.

Ethan stretched across the misty ice water. 'I can't quite reach. I need a few extra centimetres, that's all.'

Amber joined Ethan by the side of the puddle. 'Hold on to my arm,' she said. Gripping Ethan's hand, Amber leaned out as far as she could. She slipped a finger into the key ring and pulled. The clip on Storm's belt gave way with a loud twang, sending the keys skywards and Ethan lurching backwards into Lake Splashdown. Ethan looked on powerlessly as the keys arched over the deadly puddle. Gravity took hold. The keys plunged downwards. It was at that exact moment Amber dived across the puddle and snatched the keys from mid-air. She hit the ground near the door and rolled. Jumping to her feet, she threw them towards Ethan. 'Catch.'

Leaping to his feet, Ethan reached out a hand, but

they sailed straight past him and into the darkness of the cave beyond. He scrambled into the gloom at the rear of the cell.

'Hurry, Ethan. The puddle's getting bigger!' shouted Amber.

Ethan rummaged in the dark with no idea which direction the keys went, until... 'I've found them.' He stood up and bashed his head hard on the low hanging roof. 'Ow!' He crawled back to where Lake was imprisoned. The spreading pond had reached to within a couple of centimetres of Lake's feet.

'I think now would be a good time to use that key,' said Lake. Ethan rubbed his head with one hand and fumbled with the lock with the other. The locks opened one after the other, as the liquid edged ever closer. Just as the steaming pool reached the chair, Ethan managed to free the final shackle. Lake jumped over the back of the chair and took hold of Ethan's wrist, pulling him back from the edge. 'I hope you're better at long jump than you are at catch.' Lake eyed the dangerous substance that crept steadily closer. He took a few steps backwards and ran, leaping across to the safety of the door. 'OK, your turn.'

Ethan backed up as far as he could and focused on the exit. If he messed up, he was toast. He accelerated towards the puddle, his oversized trainers slapping on the cave floor. All of a sudden, he was airborne. He closed his eyes as he flew over the prone figure of Storm Floodwater and before he knew it, he crashed into Amber.

CHAPTER 11

The Emperor's Meeting

'Y ou really nailed that landing,' said Lake. He turned to his left. 'I take it you're Amber.'

Amber nodded.

Lake briefed Amber regarding the stolen fun essence, and the fun machine.

'So, it was the fun machine that gave Ethan an electric shock,' said Amber.

'We can't hang about here for long. Once somebody realises those two soldiers haven't returned, they'll send someone down here,' said Ethan.

'I agree,' said Lake. Follow me and stay close.'

Creeping up the passageway, they reached the kitchens first. A sharp eye-watering tang wafted through the open door, making Ethan cough.

'Who's there?' A woman's voice drifted out on the wave of sharp aromas. 'If that's you, Trickle,

I'll tan your backside. You know you're not supposed to be down here.'

Ethan stared at Lake in alarm. This stretch of passageway was long, straight and fairly well lit with nowhere to hide.

'If you're still there when I reach the door, young man...' The sound of feet slapping on flagstones galvanised Lake into action.

Gesturing wildly, he whispered into Amber's ear. She nodded once and then called out. 'Mrs Gurgle, it's me, Brook Backwater.'

The slapping of feet stopped. 'Oh, Brook, you're a good girl. I'll leave the emperor's lunch on the table by the door.' There was a sound of shuffling, followed by plates and cutlery being moved about. 'It's ready for you, dear. I can't stop to talk though. I have to get on.'

Lake nodded at Amber and gave her a thumbs-up, before reaching into the doorway and plucking a sandwich from the emperor's plate.

Ethan recognised the storerooms and servants quarters from his first foray into the palace, and pretty soon they passed the state rooms that had the scent of orange blossom and polish.

'Keep your eyes peeled. We're into the palace proper now,' said Lake.

Lake and the kids crept through high ceilinged corridors of polished crimson. Statues of strange sea creatures carved from shining blue sapphires stood at every corner as if guarding the palace against intruders. Lake stopped and pulled Ethan and Amber into an empty ballroom. Easing the enormous white doors shut, he put a finger to his pallid blue lips. Hurrying footsteps sounded from beyond the ballroom entrance, followed by voices.

'Do you have any idea what this meeting is about?'

'I believe it has something to do with the Fun Ultra Nebuliser but other than that, I couldn't say.'

'Then why hold the meeting in the throne room? Surely it would be better if it were held in the ministerial chambers.'

The two elementals rushed past the ballroom, their voices soon fading to faint echoes.

'We've got to get to the throne room. This sounds important,' said Lake.

'What's so important about the throne room?' Amber looked puzzled.

'They discuss the matters of the day in the ministerial chambers, such as making new laws and what have you. Any meeting held in the throne room is always about something out of the ordinary, like a declaration of war.' He opened one of the huge white doors, just wide enough to peek into the corridor. 'All clear. Follow me.'

Reaching a wide sweeping ruby staircase, Ethan could see the carved blue sea creature to the left of the steps held a newspaper. Edging closer to get a better look, he let out an involuntary gasp. 'It's us!' He fought hard to keep his voice under control as he scanned the print.

Overlander, Myles Ethan Myles, Wanted for crimes against Puddlemere.
Reward 1,000,000 puddle pounds.
Lake Splashdown captured during pitched battle!

He stared at Lake, who just shrugged.

'Get used to it. I've had to. At least they don't know about Amber's escape yet.'

Printed at the bottom of the page in large capital letters were the words

Female Overlander in captivity. All hail Emperor Monsoon.

'That's the Puddlemere Post for you. Always behind the times,' said Lake, as he gestured for the kids to follow him up the staircase. The huge archway with carvings of surfing cherubs soon came into view as they rounded the corner. Standing guard either side of the archway was a soldier in full dress uniform. Black trousers were tucked into highly polished knee-length boots. Their red tunics were belted with diamond studded scabbards and each guard wore a tall black hat that had EM Picked out in rubies on its front. The soldiers stood to attention with long black guns resting on their right shoulders. Faintly glowing glass bowls containing blue crystals stuck out at intervals along the top of each weapon.

'Oh no, that's what I was afraid of,' muttered Lake, under his breath.

'What?' mouthed Ethan.

'*Eams*. Electro Aqua Manipulators. I was trained to use them just before I defected. The best advice I can offer, is not to get in the way when one goes off.'

'My Lords, Ladies and Gentlemen, please stand for his immortal imperial majesty, Emperor Monsoon.' The sounds of scraping chairs and shuffling feet followed the announcement from the throne room.

'The meeting is about to start,' whispered Lake. 'Amber, you keep an eye out just in case anyone comes. Myles Ethan Myles, see what information you can pick up. You can hide behind the statue, near the archway.' The sound of blaring trumpets filled the corridor as Ethan slid along the wall to where a large jade octopus blocked the view of the guards. Crouching behind the marble plinth, Ethan listened as the emperor began his speech.

'My loyal subjects, we now stand on the verge of a revolution. The sun is about to rise on a new dawn. Joy and happiness shall be ours forever more.'

Cheers and applause filled the air, with the occasional whoop and whistle. When the clapping died away, the emperor continued.

'Ever since Black Funday, when the Overlanders stole our sense of enjoyment, we have made great strides to retrieve what is rightfully ours.'

Shouts of 'Hear, hear,' and 'damn them,' drifted from the throne room.

'We know about fun in the Overland world. They have a multitude of exciting activities. All of that enjoyment is had at our expense.'

Boos and hisses were followed by chants of 'Our fun, our fun, our fun.'

'As you are aware, our chief technologist, Doctor Freeze, invented the Fun Ultra Nebuliser, which takes back the fun essence from children with a highly tuned sense of enjoyment. However, due to what was believed to have been a misfire on its maiden operation, one of the two rose gold quartz batteries were destroyed. This left the fun machine running at half power.'

Murmuring drifted from the assembled crowd.

The emperor held up a hand and waited for the muttering to stop. 'It has since been discovered the quartz had been stolen by a thieving child. We have now recovered it, and our top engineers are re-fitting it into the fun machine. Once re-calibration is complete and the machine is up to full power, we will be able to suck all of the fun from the special children possessing extra strong essence. To make sure this operation is successful, we will be removing the fun from the whole of Overland just in case we miss anyone. During the powering up process, the fun machine will be running on tick-over. However, when it powers up fully, fun and enjoyment will be ours once again.'

An enormous cheer went up, with a 'Hip, hip hooray,' and 'may water bless his imperial majesty.'

Ethan turned the information over in his mind. No fun means no crazy golf or football. As grim as his mood was, he couldn't help thinking of all the other people who would lose their sense of enjoyment and what it would mean for the whole of mankind. As he slid back along the wall towards Amber and Lake, a mosquito buzzed him. Slapping it away, he rounded the corner to where Lake and Amber were waiting for him.

'Well?' asked Lake.

'The rose gold quartz is being put back into the fun machine,' said Ethan. 'This will make it run at full power. All the fun will be sucked out of our world in one go.'

'What?' Amber's eyes went wide. 'You mean no parties or sleep overs?'

Ethan could tell Amber was deep in thought. 'And, and no Christmas. The only thing on TV would be the news.'

Lake Splashdown nodded. 'That's right. If we don't do something, your world will change forever.'

'Listen, Amber.' It wasn't the right time to apologise, but Ethan knew there was a chance that they wouldn't make it out of the palace alive, so he pressed on regardless. 'I've been really nasty to you. You know. In the park. The things I said...'

She held up a hand. 'I know,' she said softly. 'I get it. You've had your fun essence stolen.' She shook her head slowly. 'I knew there was something wrong. Look, you don't have to apologise,

OK?' She gave him a brief hug. Usually he'd squirm when she got all soppy like that. Either that or suspicious. She'd either be winding him up in front of his friends, or after something. But this time it was different. He hugged her back.

'Come on, you two,' said Lake. 'We've got work to do.'

'Yeah, for sure.' Ethan let Amber go and turned to face Lake.

'We've got to find the fun machine and destroy it.' Ethan flapped a hand at the droning fly that had returned to annoy him. The gnat hovered just out of range at head height, and as Ethan took another swipe, it lit up for a split second.

'What's with that fly?' Amber's hand shot out, swatting the aggravating insect out of the air. It dropped to the polished ruby floor with a metallic clank, which made Ethan frown.

'Flies don't clank when they hit the floor.' He stooped to pick up the dead insect. 'They don't flash like cameras, either.'

'What did you just say?' Lake peered intensely at the tiny insect.

'I *said* flies don't flash like cameras.'

'It's a bug. Look closer at it,' said Lake.'

'Of course it's a bug,' said Amber, I've just swatted it.'

'You Overlanders can be so dense at times. It's a bug. A mobile camera and microphone, and if it flashed, that means it's just taken our picture. I'm hoping you killed it before the information was relayed back to the surveillance room.'

Ethan turned the bug over in his palm. The gossamer wings were connected to the body by strips of metal no wider than a human hair. Where the casing had split, Ethan could see a teeny circuit board, a tiny flywheel and two miniscule brass pistons. He moved the wings with a fingertip and watched the pistons rotate.

'Stop playing with that thing, will you? I think it's time to leave,' said Lake.

Just then, the sound of a deep gong seemed to come from everywhere at once.

'What's that noise?' Amber pushed her fingers into her ears as the air vibrated around them. Lake took hold of Amber and Ethan's hands. 'Run.'

The two soldiers guarding the archway rounded the corner. 'Stop, in the name of the emperor!' shouted one, as the second shouldered his weapon and took aim. A sizzling arc of blue light flashed down the crimson corridor, temporarily blinding Ethan. Ducking his head, he took off in what he hoped was the opposite direction and hurtled down the wide hallway.

'Stop, or I'll shoot!'

Ethan's vision cleared just in time to see a group of guards appear at the other end of the corridor. He skidded to a halt. Armed guards moved in behind him for the kill, while the soldiers ahead of him fanned out to stop his escape. Ethan looked around in desperation. He'd been separated from Lake and Amber. There was no one to help him.

'Just stay still, put your hands in the air and everything will be just fine.'

The soldier glanced to his right, just long enough to give Ethan an idea. He darted right, then left, in the direction of the stairs. Crackling bolts of light erupted from the guard's weapon, followed by an explosion of ruby fragments as Ethan dived for the staircase. Leaping down the steps three and four at a time, he could hear the yells of frustration follow him down. He ran past the statue holding the newspaper, pages rustling in his slipstream. Boots thundered on hard crystal as his pursuers took chase. Orders were barked from ahead of him. A company of soldiers were about to head him off. He'd reached the ballroom where he'd hidden with Amber and Lake. It seemed obvious, but what other choice did he have? Yanking open the tall white doors, he nipped inside and eased them shut behind him.

Leaning against the door and breathing heavily, Ethan could hear both sets of guards, and they were right outside.

'Did you see which way he went?'

'He came down the main staircase, then we lost him.'

'Have you checked this area, yet?'

'No, we arrived here the same time as you.'

'Right, well. We might as well check the ballroom out.'

CHAPTER 12

The Fun Machine

E than held his breath as the handle started to move. He quickly scanned the ballroom. A highly polished white stone floor inlaid with red diamond patterns spread out before him. At the far side of the room was a stage that stood at least two metres high. He glanced left and right but saw no steps leading from the dance floor. Anyway, he'd never make it in time, the dance floor was huge.

'Hold up a sec, I can hear someone,' said one of the guards.

Ethan felt his legs start to fold from under him. How could they have heard him? He hadn't made a sound.

'So can I. That was definitely the sound of running footsteps. We should have gone the other way. Get after the scum, go on, go.'

The door handle clicked back up, and Ethan released his breath as the sound of the guards receded down the corridor. Sinking to the floor, the reality of the situation began to dawn on him. The entire palace was searching for him, and in the chase he'd lost Amber and Lake. That meant relying on himself again.

Emptying his pockets onto the floor, he did an inventory. With all the stuff he'd picked up along the way, there was bound to be something useful that could help. Screwdriver, pliers, wire-cutters. He rummaged in his jeans and pulled out his door key, the cell keys, and the weird flying bug.

Prising the damaged casing from the mechanical fly, Ethan could clearly make out the workings. 'Hmm, positive and negative markings, just like a battery.' He poked around inside the insect's electronics and discovered a minuscule sliver of rose gold quartz. Amber must have whacked it really hard because it had been knocked clean out of its holder and was wedged against one of the wing mechanisms.

After gently prising it free, he soon worked out that the gold flecks running through the pink rock had a distinctive pattern. Rose gold quartz is a power source like a battery. If he could figure out which way round it went, he might be able to fix the bug and use it. With the pliers held steadily in his right hand, he slotted the piece of quartz into place. Nothing. Undeterred, he carefully removed it once again, turned it around, and popped it back into its holder.

The flywheel started turning, slowly at first, with a rhythmic ticking as the pistons moved back and forth. Gradually though, the speed of the little machine picked up until the pistoning wings were nothing but a blur, and the ticking became a high-pitched whine. Reaching into the guts of the electronics with the pliers, he located the switch and clicked it off. The wings slowed to a stop as the motor wound down, and he carefully put the bug into his jeans pocket.

Re-packing everything, he decided it was time to move on, so he put his ear to the door. Hearing nothing, he opened it and checked the corridor before slipping out of the ballroom. Turning right, he made his way down the wide empty passage. Every sound was amplified in this hard red space, but the sound of his breathing was soon drowned out by approaching voices. Ethan froze, as a section of wall to his right opened outwards.

Two men in white lab coats stepped into the corridor but were so deep in conversation, they failed to notice an enemy of the state standing less than three metres away. Turning their backs to Ethan, they strode down the wide concourse.

Ethan realised what he'd just seen. That was a secret door. Why have a secret door unless you've got something to hide? The lab coats too. Lab coats mean scientists and scientists mean fun machine. He'd found the fun machine by accident and wasn't about to waste an opportunity like that. The red crystal door was slowly closing. If he faffed about waiting for someone else to come out, he might never get this chance again. The technicians were only a few metres away from him, but he couldn't waste another second. If they heard him, they were hardly likely to start shooting. They were scientists, not soldiers. He broke into a crouching run and squeezed through the door, just before it swung shut with a deep thunk. He leaned back against it and breathed heavily. The passageway he was standing in was long, narrow and deep ruby, lit by strips of glowing white moonstones set at intervals along the ceiling. Creeping along the smooth red floor, he noticed that it sloped gently downwards. Light spilled from an open doorway up ahead, so he flattened himself against the wall and edged closer to the entrance.

'Bug number 43 went offline after locating the fugitives. The female Overlander struck it, but it showed signs of life about five or six minutes ago.'

'Just so long as the frequency hasn't been detuned, we might be OK. Power it up.'

Sounds of switches being clicked and hissing static drifted from the room. Ethan jumped as the tiny machine in his pocket buzzed back to life.

'I've overridden the manual shut down. We should start receiving the uploaded intel any minute now.'

'So long as the damaged bug hasn't got a broken tuner unit. If it goes off frequency, we can't get it back. Even by re-tuning the portable remote control. The bug has to be tuned to the remote. We can't do that if we don't possess it, so fingers crossed.'

Whipping the mechanical fly out of his pocket, Ethan squinted hard at the circuit board. Thinking back to the old analogue radio he'd taken to pieces to find out how it worked, he searched for the tuning device.

'We're ninety percent uploaded. If we can keep the connection for a few more seconds, we'll get the full intel. Including its location.'

Ethan fished in his pocket for the needle nosed pliers.

'Ninety eight percent. We're nearly there.'

Gripping the pliers in his trembling fingers, Ethan pushed the pointed end into the tuner's slot.

'Ninety nine percent. We'll soon have the info.'

Ethan turned the pliers in the slot.

'Ninety-nine point eight. Come on, one more second. Oh damn.' The sound of a fist hitting a desk was followed by shouts of frustration. 'We've lost the connection. The portable remote is now useless. I told Doctor Freeze about the design flaw, but he never listens. He just threatens to have me hosed with hyperthermium.'

Putting the bug and the pliers back into his pocket, Ethan crouched as low as he could and peeked into the room. A row of wall mounted monitors overlooked a polished black marble control desk full of switches, buttons and flashing lights.

Next to the control desk was a bank of hand-held remote controls, each the size of a mobile phone. Created from a single piece of machined quartz, each remote had a small screen that looked as though it were made from a perfectly squared piece of flint. Two technicians stared down at one of these remotes that had been wired up to some kind of computer. An oversized keyboard, reminding Ethan of an antique typewriter, was connected to one of the monitors. Fat metal hoses snaked from the keyboard to the screen with one of the smaller hoses plugged into the remote.

'Unplug it. It's no use now. We've lost the connection.' The taller scientist shook his head.

The smaller of the two pulled on the metal hose that connected to the remote. It came off with a sucking pop and flopped onto the desk. 'I'll put the remote back into its charging cradle. We can set it up for one of the spare bugs.' He turned towards the door, and Ethan ducked back out of sight.

If he could get the remote, maybe he could operate the spy bug and use it for recon. Risking a look, Ethan poked his head around the door. They had their backs to him and were busy typing on the huge clunky keyboard. Ethan knew that if he waited too long, he'd get discovered. There was only one way to do it and that was to do it. He took a deep breath, left the cover of the doorway and slipped into the little room. His luck was holding. Both technicians had their backs to him, so he took a second step. He reached out a hand to grab the remote and froze. The taller technician had stopped typing. Something was wrong, very wrong. Lowering his hand, he backed out of the room as quietly as he could. The Puddle person was slowly turning around. Ethan pulled back from the doorway into the corridor but scraped his foot against the door frame.

'Did you hear something?'

'Only the humming of the generators. Why?'

'I could have sworn someone was in the room with us.'

'You're just worried Doctor Freeze will come down for a spot check.'

'Yes, I suppose you're right. Anyway, what was the final part of that algorithm, again?'

With his pulse thundering in his ears, Ethan decided to give it one last go. He wiped his sweaty palms on his damp jeans and peeped into the room. Both scientists had gone back to their task on the computer and had their backs to him, once again. This was his chance. Not daring to breathe, he eased himself into the claustrophobic red space and once more stretched a hand for the remote. Was he pushing his luck just that bit too far? He sincerely hoped not. He plucked the remote from its cradle and backed towards the doorway. He was almost out of the room when the tall elemental wheeled around.

'I knew it!' he yelled. 'Raise the alarm. It's the Overlander.' The scientist lunged for Ethan but froze mid-stride. Recognising the onset of another blast of fun essence, Ethan turned and fled down the crimson corridor.

Not knowing how long this burst was going to last, meant Ethan didn't know how long he had before the alarm was raised. He ran on until the smooth ruby gave way to rough-hewn rock. The passageway widened, and the low ceiling soared away into the shadows overhead. As he rounded a wide bend, he slowed to a stop. Up ahead was a huge steel door, lit by a vast array of glowing white moonstone floodlights. The door was so big, it could have been an aircraft hangar for a Jumbo Jet. Painted on the door in metre high letters, was a warning:

Fun Machine.
No Unauthorised Entry – Trespassers Will Be Frozen.

Melting back into the shadows, Ethan surveyed the area. A normal sized door opened into the hangar door, but he would never be able to reach it without being seen. There were two guard towers, one either side of the hangar entrance. Pulling the bug and remote control out of his jeans pocket, he set to work re-tuning the device. He could fly it up to the watch towers to see if there was anything he could do to distract the guards just long enough to sneak into the hangar.

Placing the whining spy bug on the floor, he rested his thumbs on the two smooth amethyst buttons protruding from the remote-control board. With gentle movements, he soon had the buzzing drone under control and watched as it hummed out of the shadows into the floodlit brightness. The square black screen crackled to life, like a phone screen. It was made from polished flint and showed a bugs-eye view of the right-hand watch tower.

Ethan hovered the spy bug over the head of the watchman and scanned the area. Just like Storm Floodwater, the guard was armed with a therm cannon. Ethan lowered the bug to inspect the vat of hyperthermium. A vale of mist hovered ghostly white over the surface of the deadly liquid. Unsure how he was going to cause a distraction, Ethan buzzed the gnat aimlessly around the legs of the frosted container until he spotted something.

'Gotcha.' A small drainage tap was located at the base of the container. Hidden from view by the falling curtain of icy mist, he was lucky to have seen it at all. A long wooden lever stuck out from the main body of the tap. Beside it was a sign reading; *Warning - Always connect drainage hose before opening valve.*

A plan formulated in his mind. He'd have to act fast if he were to succeed. Reversing the spy bug as far as it would go in the cramped watch tower, Ethan aligned the drone with the wooden lever. With a burst of acceleration, he crashed it headlong into the valve handle. A clunk followed by a creak came from the small speaker in the handset.

'What's that?' The watch tower guard's puzzled expression wavered into view from behind the misty curtain, just as a deathly stream gushed from the drainage valve. Yelps and curses flew, as the guard tried frantically to turn the tap off.

'Oy, Drench, are you OK?' called the second watchman.

By now, the floor of the lookout platform was completely soaked in hyperthermium, freezing watchman Drench to the floor.

'Of course I'm not OK! Get over here, will you! The pigging valve's busted and flooded the place. I'm stuck fast up here.'

Ethan flew the bug across to the far side of the hangar and into the other watch tower. He had to stop the second watchman from leaving, or his plan would fail. Thinking on his feet, he aimed straight for the guard's left eye. It contacted with a wet smack.

'Ow, ow, ow!' The watchman dropped to his knees, pressing a hand to his face.

'Here, Slosh! Are you coming to help, or not? I'm frozen up to my knees, now.'

Slosh just knelt on the floor and moaned in pain, as Ethan lined up the spy bug with the drainage tap. With a sharp crack, the valve snapped clean off, sending the bug spinning out of control and into the stream of lethal fluid. The screen on the small hand-held remote went blank, but not before Ethan caught a glimpse of watchman Slosh twinkling white with frost.

He'd lost the spy bug, but it didn't matter. He'd neutralised the guard towers. Now all he had to do was find a way in. The entrance to the hangar was at least two hundred metres away and bathed in hard white light. He'd be exposed, but he had no choice. The fun machine, and probably his fun essence were on the other side of that door. Leaving the cover of the shadows, he sprinted out into the open.

As he neared the enormous hangar entrance, he made for the smaller person-sized door. He'd almost reached his goal when the small door opened outwards. He had to think fast if he didn't want to get caught. The entrance swung wide, just as he swerved hard to the right. Getting this wrong would land him on Doctor Freeze's operating table, so he'd better not foul things up. He slid in behind the door, just as it opened fully, covering him from view. He'd seen the move in plenty of films but never thought it would actually work. Two engineers exited and strolled out into the wide brightness. So long as they didn't look back, he just might get away with it. Wasting no time, he crept around the closing door and slipped through the entrance.

Ethan didn't have any idea what could be inside the hangar, but what he looked at right now was beyond his wildest imaginings. A vast cavern had been carved out of the rock and sitting in the centre was the strangest apparatus he'd ever seen.

It was shaped like a human heart and beat with a steady rhythm. The metallic skin expanded and contracted as if the thing was a living, breathing entity and at every pulse, highly polished flywheels rotated, powered by enormous pistons. A complicated array of copper pipes twisted this way and that, vibrating and clanking at every beat, and at the top of the strange machine, perched a satellite dish. A bright green light pulsed from the centre of the dish in perfect sync with the heart-like rhythm. This was it. He'd found the fun machine. An involuntary shiver passed through him as he stared at the invention that was going to drain the entire human race of enjoyment.

Puddle people were everywhere. Up ladders, adjusting valves on the fun machine and taking samples from the stream running through the middle of the room. Ethan assumed they were Puddle people, but he couldn't be entirely sure, as they were all wearing old fashioned diving suits with big brass helmets. Pretty soon he understood why. The heat given off by the massive contraption filled the air with an uncomfortable, tropical swelter. The suits must be personal air conditioners.

He ducked out of sight behind a stack of packing crates and pondered what to do next.

That was when he spotted an elaborate clock, mounted high on the fun machine's side. Intricately carved Roman numerals sat in a face of polished brass. Springs wound in and out at every click of the bejewelled second hand, and a square slot with the words *days, hours, minutes* and *seconds*, counted steadily down towards zero. When the clock clicked over to one hour and thirty minutes, a horn sounded, filling the fetid steamy air with thunderous noise.

'Ninety minutes until power-up. I repeat, ninety minutes until power-up.'

The amplified voice echoed around the stone chamber, causing everyone to stop what they were doing and look up. A wave of cool air wafted over Ethan, as the two white coated technicians re-entered the chamber.

'The switch over is in an hour and a half. I can't believe it's actually happening,' said the first Puddle person.

Ethan sunk further behind the packing crates and listened intently.

'Oh yes. It will be a glorious day for Puddlemere. The calibrations are nearly complete. It's just a case of double checking the numbers then throwing the switch at the exact moment.'

Ethan looked through a gap between the cases. The two technicians stood by a row of grey metal lockers.

'It won't be long. All of our stolen fun will be back where it belongs.'

Ethan watched as the Puddle people pulled two suits out of the lockers.

They poured themselves into the neck holes and

secured the bulky brass helmets with a sturdy clonk.

'Best we go and check the latest batch of essence.'

The voice came from the tinny speaker mounted behind a grille on the front of the helmet. The second elemental nodded in agreement, and they headed off towards the tall racks of metal shelving. Keeping to the shadows, Ethan followed the two scientists until they reached the wall of racking. Each shelf was filled with row after row of small crystal vials. A bright orange liquid filled each vial, and the sign which hung above the racking read; *Warning - Concentrated Fun Essence. Harmful If Swallowed.*

It was all very well finding his and Amber's fun essence, but how was he going to retrieve it without getting caught?

CHAPTER 13

The Countdown Begins

T he horn blared once more. 'This is an announcement for all residents of Puddlemere,' said the amplified voice. 'His majesty, Emperor Monsoon, has decreed that everybody is to gather at the steps of the ruby palace for the fun machine powering up ceremony. Anybody found to be absent without a good reason will be severely punished.'

Ethan glanced up to where the voice had sounded from. He noticed that there were a couple of chiselled square rocks with polished copper pipes leading from them. Suddenly they crackled to life again, making him jump.

'Your attention, please. Myles Ethan Myles has been spotted in the vicinity of the fun machine passageway. Be warned, he is thought to be armed and dangerous. This ends transmission.'

Armed and dangerous? He was only eleven and

definitely not armed. He thought about the guards with therm guns. They'd be shooting on sight from now on. He crept back to the stack of packing crates and huddled down behind them. He was trying to figure out what to do next, when he heard a voice from the other side of the cases.

'I'm taking a breather.'

A suited-up technician stomped into view, and Ethan sunk further into the shadows. The Puddle person twisted the brass helmet off, turned himself into water and cascaded out of the neck hole. He reverted to person-form and hung the baggy brown suit in a locker, along with the helmet. A rush of cool air chilled the sweat on Ethan's brow as the worker exited the facility.

Ethan stared at the locker as an idea started forming. If he could grab one of those diving suits, he could walk around without being noticed. Once he'd put the brass helmet on, nobody would know it was him. He'd be hiding in plain sight. He lifted his head just far enough over the boxes to have a look around.

Nobody seemed to notice as he opened the locker and lifted out the diving suit. He pulled the garment down into his hiding place and looked for the zip. When he didn't find one, he thought about how the operative managed to get out of the cumbersome outfit. He'd got out through the neck hole. He looked at the brass locking ring, laid the diving suit on the floor and wriggled into it. It was even harder to get into than the wetsuit he'd worn during last summer's trip to Cornwall. Both legs had gone in without a hitch, but he was now stuck fast at the hips. He squirmed and bucked. No matter how big the locking ring was, it just wasn't big enough.

'Rinse, is that you?'

Ethan stopped wriggling and squinted through sweat-stung eyes. The Puddle person was just the other side of the packing cases, and there *he* was half in and half out of one of their suits, stuck fast.

'Come on, Rinse, we've got work to do.'

Ethan had to do something to get rid of this guy, but what? If he didn't say something, the elemental would walk around the cases, and he'd be so busted. He had to disguise his voice somehow. He cupped a hand across his mouth and in as low a voice as he could muster, he muttered, 'give us a minute.' His nerves jangled as he waited for a reply. He hoped his ruse had worked. It was loud in the fun machine cavern, so maybe, just maybe, he'd get away with it.

'OK, just don't be long, all right?'

The sound of footsteps clumping away from him made Ethan shake his head in disbelief. He'd done it again. He'd got away with it. Surely his luck was due to run out, soon? Nobody could be this lucky, could they? He resumed his fight to get into the suit and twisted and writhed until the back pocket of his jeans ripped clean off, and he popped down through the brass ring.

As soon as he clicked it into place, the helmet

filled with a low humming sound, and the temperature dropped from Amazonian high summer, to British springtime. The energy seeped back into him as the cool air circulated. Re-invigorated, he stepped out into the vast chamber and hoped he wouldn't get caught out.

'Ah, Rinse Reservoir. Just the person to help me with some calibrations.'

The engineer stepped up to Ethan and thrust a clipboard into his hands.

'With just over an hour before power up, I wanted to be sure the second rose gold quartz is properly calibrated. I know it's been done a dozen times already, but I just need to be sure. We can't be too cautious, can we?'

Ethan looked down at the clipboard, hoping the engineer hadn't noticed his face through the glass plate of the helmet. He'd just been asked a question about, what was it again? Calibration, or something? He had to reply, but the worry about being found out had stressed him so much, he couldn't quite remember what the question was. He took a gamble and shook his head. The engineer continued his conversation.

'If the numbers on the chart are correct, the upgraded machine will be capable of amazing things.'

Relief flooded through Ethan. Obviously, he had answered correctly. He looked up to see the worker walk over towards a brass panel on the fun machine and flick it up.

Behind the shiny cover were a row of polished brass taps with melted glass pendulums dangling from them. Each hanging blob pulsed with tiny red lights.

'Does the read-out correspond with the chart? I think it does, but I just want to be certain.'

Ethan glanced down at the clipboard. The algebra was so complicated, it made his head swim.

'I wanted to be sure about the synchronisation. The sine wave looks right, so what do you think the numbers should be?'

A clueless Ethan pretended to study the clipboard and flashing red lights. If he said anything at all, he'd be found out. Even if by some miracle he guessed the correct number, he'd still be found out, as he definitely was not Rinse Reservoir. He was convinced his luck had run its course, until he remembered Martin Jones. The whole class had to memorise a passage from Shakespeare and read it aloud, one by one. Martin hadn't bothered but still got away with it by feigning tonsillitis. Ethan pointed to his throat, shook his head and shrugged.

'This is a staff announcement.'

The speakers whistled with feedback for a couple of seconds, before the voice continued.

'Will Lagoon please come to the nebuliser induction pipe, immediately.'

With a sound like frying bacon, the microphone switched off.

'Sorry to hear about your sore throat, old chap. Sounds like dehydration to me.'

Ethan spotted the name tag on the guy's breast pocket. *Lagoon, Nebuliser Engineer - First Class.*

'Gotta go,' said Lagoon. 'Let me have your thoughts on those numbers as soon as possible, won't you?'

As Lagoon strode away, Ethan pressed a palm to his thundering heart. His mouth was so dry, he felt as though he'd swallowed sand, and his throat made a funny clicking noise when he swallowed. He staggered slightly on wobbly legs, hoping that nobody noticed. With the clipboard in his hand, he walked around the fun machine, stopping every once in a while to look down at the complicated mathematics and then back up towards the beating, heart-shaped contraption. That's when he spotted it. At the top of the fun machine was a small yellow sign that read

Rose Gold Quartz – Handle With Care.

A tower of metal scaffolding was set up to give access to what was essentially the off button, but there was no way Ethan could reach it without giving himself away. Engineers and technicians swarmed over the ladders and platforms. One opened the access hatch to the quartz and shone a small torch inside. All he had to do was keep walking. Now he knew where the rose gold quartz was, he'd be able to stop the insanity. First of all, however, he had to get his and Amber's fun.

❖ ❖ ❖

The metal racks holding the vials were much taller than Ethan had realised. They stretched into the upper reaches of the steamy hollow, their tops lost to sight. He stood at the base of the huge ladder and stared upwards. How was he going to find his and Amber's essence? There had to be at least ten thousand glowing orange vials. He picked one from the shelves at random. Engraved on the glass was the name Susan Rowbottom. Putting it back, he reached above his head and plucked another glowing vial. Patrick O'Brian. The one next to it read Patricia Laing. He scanned the rows. The tiny crystal bottles were arranged alphabetically. The ladder he stood next to connected to the racking and slid along on rails, enabling access to any essence required. Ethan manoeuvred the steps to where he thought his essence would be and climbed as fast as the heavy air-conditioned suit would allow. 'Got it.' He looked around. There was nobody anywhere near him, so he twisted the big brass helmet and lifted it off. There was a gentle hiss as the helmet separated from the locking ring, and the stifling heat rushed in.

After the cool comfort of the personal air-conditioning unit, Ethan found the soupy air difficult to breathe. Sweat blurred his vision as he reached for the little container. Grasping the small bottle, he pulled the cork out with his teeth and hesitated. The warning sign had something on it about this stuff being dangerous to swallow. He sniffed the contents. A rush of tangerine scented enjoyment made his head spin. Hooking an arm through one of the rungs, he held on tightly, as silver and gold stars burst at the edge of his vision. He stared at the orange potion for a second, tipped his head back and gulped it down. It slid down his throat until it hit his stomach, where it lay like a pool of lead. Frowning, he put the empty vial back on the shelf and replaced the helmet.

Why hadn't anything happened? He descended the ladder. Just as his feet touched the floor, he felt a prickling in the tips of his fingers, which rapidly seeped throughout the whole of his body. This was followed by what he could only describe as a taste explosion. One after another, his favourite flavours flowed over his tongue until he dribbled uncontrollably. Thoughts of football, remote controlled gadgets, and Amber's ninth birthday party filled his head with such rapture, he felt like whooping.

Remembering where he was, he pushed the enjoyment down inside himself. There would be plenty of time for that once this was over. He repositioned the ladder and stomped to the top. He scanned the 'A' section, reading as fast as he could, until he spotted Amber's vial, just within reach. Before he could snatch the glowing bottle from the shelf, the speakers squealed back to life.

'Attention. Myles Ethan Myles has been spotted in the A section of the fun essence racking.' The microphone crackled before the voice came back on. 'The fugitive is to be taken alive if possible, but the use of force, if necessary, has been approved. End transmission.'

He'd been wondering when his run of luck would come to an end. Well, this was it. He'd been spotted, and the worst thing was the fact that he was thirty feet off the ground at the top of a ladder.

He stretched out a hand to grab Amber's essence and felt the ladder bounce as if somebody had stepped onto it. He glanced down, and to his horror saw a helmeted technician climbing up towards him. He didn't have anywhere to escape to. He couldn't go up, and he definitely couldn't go down. He did the only thing he could and leaned out one more time to grab Amber's essence. If he was about to get caught, the least he could do was to get what he came for. His fingers brushed the tiny bottle just as the ladder jounced violently. He'd over-reached, and the sudden movement tipped his balance beyond recovery. He slid sideways, hands grasping empty air. There was no way he was escaping his fate this time. He was going to hit a solid rock floor at terminal velocity, and all he had to protect himself was a brass helmet. A fat lot of good that would do if the rest of his body had been pulverised.

Unable to close his eyes, he watched in mute terror as the ground rushed up to meet him. A violent jerk wrenched him sideways, and the helmet clanged against the metal racking.

His fall had been halted. He was still alive. But how? He twisted his head around as far as it would go. The oversized suit had snagged on the corner of the shelving. With his right foot still caught in the top rung of the ladder, he dangled like a broken puppet. Elementals had started gathering below him. They pointed up at him and gestured wildly to each other. It didn't matter what happened next, he was going to die, no matter what. Either he'd crash to the ground or get rescued and have his brain cut out. Some choice! That's when he felt the material of the suit start to give.

A small tear was followed by a whoosh, as the cool air rushed out of the hole into the steamy atmosphere. Ethan jolted downwards as the small tear lengthened. With a sound like Velcro, the rip opened wide, spilling Ethan out into space. He squeezed his eyes shut and waited for the impact. But instead of being bashed to pieces on the stone floor, he landed headfirst in a tepid pool. The upward explosion of water re-formed itself into six elementals, who hit the floor running. He was outnumbered, but he was smaller and hopefully faster. Leaping to his feet, he took off across the huge cavern and caught a glimpse of flashing orange out of the corner of his eye. Amber's vial had been knocked loose and now plummeted towards the ground. He put on a burst of speed, dodging past the grasping hands of one elemental, only to be tripped by another. As his feet left the floor, he could see the small vial spinning through the air ahead of him. He stretched a hand in a last-ditch effort to save his sister's fun, hit the floor and forward rolled. Springing to his feet again, he ran on, his lungs heaving in the heavy air. He'd failed. Amber would be miserable for the rest of her life, and it was all his fault. If he hadn't insisted on having a closer look at the puddle portal, none of this would have happened.

He realised he was gripping something in his fist. He risked a glance. An orange glow filtered through the gap in his fingers. He was astonished to discover Amber's fun essence gripped tightly in his palm. His adrenalin had been pumping so hard, he hadn't realised he'd caught the little bottle. He stuffed it into his pocket. His feeling of elation, however, was short lived. He'd reached the fast-flowing stream that ran through the middle of the cave. Too wide to jump and too fast to dive into, he realised he was trapped.

'It's over. You may as well come quietly. We've called the guards. They'll be here with therm guns any second now. Give up and you'll be unharmed.' They had him surrounded. He couldn't go forwards or backwards. His eyes flicked from the churning river to the Puddle people. He couldn't just give up. He'd come too far for that. He'd got his fun back, saved Amber's essence and discovered how to disable the fun machine. Give up? He shook his head slowly. 'No,' he said quietly and rushed headlong at the group of workers, feigned left and darted right. A blur of water rushed at him with surprising speed, blasting him in the chest like a fire hose. He hit the ground and scurried backwards away from the onslaught. The vicious jet reformed itself into an elemental.

Ethan heaved himself upright and lifted his fists.

'You just don't give up, do you?' The head engineer advanced, swaying gently from side to side like a cobra about to strike. Ethan lurched forwards, swinging wildly and connected with air. The punch to the side of his head sent him reeling towards the rushing stream. A hand clamped his shoulder and spun him round. 'I've got you now. You're coming with me.'

Acting purely on impulse, Ethan reared back and slammed his forehead into his opponent's nose. A wet crunch was followed by a howl of pain. The Puddle person staggered backwards, hand over his face. Water gushed from between his fingers and splashed on the rocky ground, like clear blood.

The technicians parted, as a troop of six armed guards ran through their midst.

'Lock your fingers behind your head and kneel on the ground!' shouted one of the soldiers. 'Do it now!' he yelled and pointed his rifle at Ethan's head. Ethan raised his hands slowly and stumbled. A sizzling flash lit the air above him as he fell backwards into the churning stream. The rushing torrent swallowed him, dragging him down. He fought to keep his head above the hot spume, but the current was too strong for him. Staring up, he could see hands reaching for him, but it was no use. With no more air in his body, he heaved in a shuddering breath, expecting to drown. Water rushed into his lungs, but to his amazement, he found that he could still breathe. It was the puddle draught. He'd forgotten all about it. It enabled him to breathe under water. That was something the fun machine workers didn't know. At least, he hoped they didn't know. A rough plan had popped into his head to stop them looking for him. If he faked his own death, pretended to drown, then they'd have no use for him and no reason to search for him.

He jerked and twisted, thrashing his arms and legs and then went still. He wasn't entirely sure he'd made it look convincing, he just hoped they had fallen for it. He breathed out, allowing his body to sink and the current to carry him downstream.

The river gradually cooled as it passed through a twisting network of caves. Caverns of glittering white floated by, as Ethan was washed through them. He passed rooms filled with blue and green gemstones and strange shaped rocks that looked like alligators and prowling tigers. On and on he floated until the river slowed to a stop. The hot chemical tang of the fun machine cavern had been replaced with something more familiar. The smell of rotting wood and old engine oil filled the air. He swam towards the dull grey light of the exit and squinted as he emerged from under a derelict factory. He knew exactly where he was. He knew that smell and recognised the sooted remains of the long dead gantries and cranes. It took him a minute or so to get his bearings, but when he did, he set off with renewed vigour towards the Dryads' hideout.

He stopped when a loud buzzing sounded from overhead. This was followed by an amplified voice. 'Your attention please,' said the disembodied voice. 'One hour before fun machine power up. I repeat. One hour before fun machine power up. Transmission ends.'

He bobbed in the water. In sixty minutes the whole of mankind was going to be drained of all enjoyment. He shook his head. He'd never do it in time. Despair swamped his sense of enjoyment as he swam dejectedly towards the disused mill. One hour. One measly hour.

CHAPTER 14

The Plan

Ethan pulled himself up through the hole and into the Dryads' hideout. He clambered to his feet and trudged down the entrance tunnel.

'Myles Ethan Myles! said Lake Splashdown, as Ethan entered the chamber. 'Thank water you're safe. I thought I'd never see you again after we got separated.'

The meeting room was packed. On the round table was a detailed diagram depicting the palace.

'The fun machine,' said Ethan. 'We've got less than an hour before it sucks all the fun from Overland.'

'We know,' said Lake. 'That's one of two problems we're trying to solve.'

Ethan looked around the chamber and frowned. 'Is Amber in the guest room?'

'That's the other problem.'

'What do you mean?'

'She was recaptured during the shootout with the palace guards,' said Lake. 'As good as I am at unarmed combat, I'm no match for therm guns.'

'Amber's been captured again?' He couldn't believe what he was hearing. Not only were they nearly out of time, but his sister was back in the hands of that frozen freak.

'She's safe for now. You remember Brook Backwater, our palace spy?'

Ethan nodded.

'She's keeping an eye on her. Amber's being held in the throne room ante-chamber which, for now, is good news.'

'Why?'

'Well,' said Lake. 'It means she hasn't caught the interest of Doctor Freeze and that can only be a good thing.' Lake turned to the assembled crowd. 'Is everybody clear about the rescue plan?'

'Yes, Commander,' said one of the Dryads. 'We're to mingle with the crowd outside the palace gates and start a riot as a distraction.'

'That's right, Wave. When the guards come running, I'll slip into the service entrance near the anteroom during the confusion. I'll put on a stolen uniform and rescue Amber. So long as nobody looks too closely, I'll be able to pass as a palace guard. I'll take Amber to the cell in the ruby dungeons and get her out through the secret exit.'

'But the fun machine needs to be broken,' said Ethan. 'Otherwise my entire world will lose its essence.'

Eldermaster Rain, who had been sitting quietly the whole time, stood up and cleared his throat. 'Myles Ethan Myles, we wish we could help you, but we don't know where the fun machine is. Lake Splashdown defected before that damned thing was built and our spies have been unable to locate it.'

'I know where it is. I found it by accident.' Ethan pointed excitedly at the map. 'There's a secret door near the ballroom. There's also a fast-flowing stream they use to cool the fun machine. The stream comes out under one of the old warehouses, near here.'

'This is good news, and it changes everything.' The eldermaster rose to his feet.

'The rescue team are going to have to be strong swimmers to go against the current. It's really powerful,' said Ethan.

'Good thinking.' Eldermaster Rain turned to face Lake Splashdown. 'Pick the strongest and leave the weakest here. It'll reduce the risk of collateral damage.'

Ethan removed the bottle of fun essence from his jeans pocket and gave it to Lake. 'It's Amber's. Please take good care of it. She'll need to take it as soon as possible to keep her spirits up.'

'Don't worry, I will. I'll also give her a flask of puddle draught. She'll need to keep up her strength, as well. Anyway, before we crack on, I need to show you something.' Lifting a pile of papers from the round table, he handed Ethan the top sheet.

'I don't understand. What's this?' Ethan frowned.

'Read the heading,' said Lake.

'Earth elemental re-animation experiment No. 13. What's that, then?'

'It's the experiment Doctor Freeze was working on that caused Black Funday. The explosion, the release of dangerous gasses, and the fun that Puddlemere lost. It's all in there. This is the proof that will be Doctor Freeze's undoing. He even detailed how he would blame your people for stealing our fun, therefore justifying building the fun machine. In a footnote on page twenty-five, he called the emperor a *gullible fool* for believing him. Such loyalty, eh?'

'Where did you get this paperwork?' asked Ethan.

'After I stole the uniform to use as a disguise,' said Lake, 'I had a root around in Doctor Freeze's lab. It's in a hell of a mess down there, by the way. What did you do to it? Anyway, behind the partition wall there's a cupboard with a sticky handle. It was on a shelf in there.'

Ethan thought for a moment. 'I hid in that cupboard with Amber when Drip and Drizzle came in to see Doctor Freeze.'

'So, you know where I mean, then. Anyway, I nabbed the paperwork just before the guards burst in. Right now, though, I need the bunch of keys you took from Storm Floodwater.'

'Yeah, of course,' said Ethan.

Lake picked through the keys until he found what he was looking for. 'Here's the ante-room key. I'll use it to free Amber.'

'What about the fun machine?' asked Ethan.

'Good thinking. Once Amber is in my care, Brook Backwater will be free to launch a frontal attack along with agent Trickle, whilst the team swim upstream to launch a rear-guard action.'

'Why do we have to do all of this?' asked Ethan. 'Why not just take Doctor Freeze's documents straight to the emperor?'

'You are on the ball today. It must be the puddle draught making your brain work properly,' said Lake. 'Getting documents to his eminence takes time we don't have, right now. Certain protocols have to be followed. It could take weeks.'

Lake picked up a two handled stoneware cup, drained the contents, then banged it twice on the table. 'Listen up, everyone!' he shouted.

The chattering died down and Lake stepped onto the tabletop. 'What I'm asking of you all today is not an easy thing to do. Puddlemere enjoyment has been had at the expense of an entire race. A race blamed for the mistakes of one irresponsible elemental. Doctor Freeze was willing to condemn Myles Ethan Myles's people to an existence of everlasting misery. We cannot allow that to happen. Search your conscience and you will see I'm right. If we succeed, then all humans shall be free to bask in the fun and enjoyment that's rightfully theirs. If we fail, though, they will be plunged into a new dark age, made worse by the doctor's evil and twisted science. We must be willing to sacrifice our own enjoyment for the sake of doing the honourable thing. We don't do these things because they are easy. We do them because they are right.'

Cheering reverberated around the cavern, and Lake jumped from the table.

'Let's go,' said Ethan.

Lake frowned. 'You're staying here. You could have been killed when you broke into the palace last time.'

'If it wasn't for me, you could have been killed.'

Lake sighed. 'And I'm eternally grateful, but this time I've got back-up. There's no point in putting you at risk.'

'This is about your brother, isn't it?'

Lake nodded. 'So, you heard the conversation between me and Storm, then?'

'Something about ghost glass. You don't want me to get hurt. I get it, but I can't just sit around when my own sister is in danger.'

'I understand that. Doctor Freeze sent my brother to his death, and there was nothing I could do about it.'

'In that case, let me come with you.'

Lake paused for a moment before continuing. 'I

tell you what. I'll need help at the secret cave. The one we landed in when we first escaped. Meet me there, OK?'

Ethan nodded.

'We'd better leave now. We've only got twenty minutes before the fun machine powers up to full strength.'

Lake and Ethan swam in silence through the waterways of the old industrial zone. Stale smelling water lapped at the rotten posts of long forgotten piers and jetties.

'This is where I have to leave you,' said Lake. 'I'll be as quick as I can.'

They'd reached the little stone beach leading to the secret passage. Ethan waded ashore and turned to face Lake. 'Save Amber,' he said, before squeezing through the fissure in the rock.

He went over the plan in his head. A whole team of Dryads were working to destroy the fun machine and Lake was on his way to save Amber. He knew all of this, but he was still anxious. He paced around the dank little cave unable to settle. He realised, now, that he'd been sent here just to make it feel like he was being useful. Well, he *was* useful. Who was it that discovered the location of the fun machine? Who saved Lake from Storm Floodwater? If it wasn't for him, the Dryads wouldn't even *have* a mission. That made his mind up. He was going up that drainage pipe into the palace, one more time. He was as much a part of this as anybody.

He jumped up and grabbed the lip of the stone pipe. He'd done this before, he could do it again. The climb back to the prison cell wasn't any easier this time around, but eventually he made it to the top.

Easing the manhole cover off, he pulled himself up through the hole. The hyperthermium had, thankfully, evaporated leaving Drizzle and Drip as permanent ice sculptures. The canister lay on its side, its two good legs sticking out like antennae.

'Overlander,' croaked Storm Floodwater. He crouched on the floor looking battle worn, his frozen right hand still gripping the useless weapon. 'Can't keep away, is that it?'

Ethan hugged the wall and shuffled around to the cell door, not taking his eyes from the immobile Sergeant.

'I suppose you got a special invite to the fun machine powering up ceremony,' said Storm. 'Come to watch as your thieving race get their fun taken back off them.'

Ethan tried to ignore the taunts as he fiddled with the handle. He gripped the doorknob with shaking hands and turned. There was a loud clunk. Spinning around, he glimpsed a blur of metal as the therm cannon caught him hard on the side of the head. With an explosion of pain, he staggered backwards. Another blow sent him sprawling on the rough stone floor.

As Ethan's blurred vision cleared, he could see that Storm's right leg ended just below the knee in a shard-like stump. Had Storm severed his own frozen leg just to attack him? How desperate *was* this guy? Storm Floodwater loomed over him, his jowly face a mix of agony and triumph.

'I've got you now,' he growled.

CHAPTER 15

The Final Countdown

Ethan tried to clamber to his feet, but Storm Floodwater pushed him back down with the tip of the cannon.

'No you don't,' said Storm. 'This is all your fault.' He gestured to his frozen arm and legs. 'I'll never get my promotion now.' Reaching down to his left ankle, Storm pulled out a tiny pistol. The glass barrel glinted in the guttering torch light. 'Luckily for you, I couldn't reach this when I was still frozen. He pointed the gun at Ethan's head. 'Luck has just run out for you and all of your fun thieving race.'

'Humans didn't steal your fun, it was Doctor Freeze!' Ethan's life now depended on him making Storm see the truth.

'Not only a thief, but a liar as well. It hardly surprises me, though.'

'It's true, we've got proof. Lake Splashdown

found the doctor's notes that were all about a failed experiment. That's what caused your fun essence to evaporate. It wasn't us. We didn't even know you existed.'

'The whole of Puddlemere knows the truth about you people. Your fun has been seeping out of you for years. All of the dreadful things you do to each other. The wars, the fights. You even hit each other for sport. I think you people call it boxing. You stole our fun to top up your own failing essence.' He pressed a small button, and Ethan's hair crackled with static.

Ethan flinched, the muscles in his neck going rigid. He squeezed his eyes shut, as a sizzling bang erupted in the enclosed space. The sharp acrid smell of lightning-fried-air filled the room, and a girl screamed.

The first thing he saw when he opened his eyes, was Amber standing in the open doorway. She looked at him with fear-filled eyes.

'Lake Splashdown. I might have known,' said Storm Floodwater, ignoring Amber.

'Diving in front of the boy to save his life. How noble.' Lake leapt to his feet and winced in pain. A large gash had been torn through his left shoulder, and his arm hung limp by his side.

'Get behind me!' he shouted at Ethan. With a whoosh, he transformed into a spinning whirlpool and advanced on Storm Floodwater.

The whirling column of water struck the pistol and sent it flying, but not before Storm managed to squeeze off another shot. A scream of pain sounded from the twisting jet of water, as a blue bolt of electricity punched through it. The gun flew through the air, hitting the back of the cave. It exploded in a shower of sparks, sending a cascade of rocks tumbling to the ground.

Lake transformed back into human shape once more. A hole had been blown through his left side and water ran out of it, forming a small pool at his feet.

'That just about makes us even.' Storm lifted his left fist.

'It doesn't have to be this way,' said Lake. 'They're innocent. It was all Freeze's doing.'

'That's exactly what the brat said. Why should I believe a lying Dryad and a thieving human?' He jabbed his fist at Lake. 'Why do you love the Overlanders so much, after all they've done to us?'

Ethan edged along the wall towards the door, not taking his eyes from the circling opponents. The secret exit had been buried under a pile of rocks, so there was no use going that way.

'For heaven's sake, move it!' shrieked Amber.

Storm Floodwater glanced at Amber just long enough for Lake to strike a blow. A clear fist landed in the middle of Storm's face. A sharp crack was followed by a grunt of pain.

The hiss of static from the palace speaker system made the two men pause for a split second.

'Five minutes until fun machine power up. I repeat. Five minutes until fun machine power up.'

Ethan and Amber's eyes locked.

'Brook and Trickle have failed,' said Ethan. 'It's down to us, now.'

'Get back here!' Storm bellowed.

'Run!' shouted Lake. 'Go to the fun machine. Your whole world is depending on you.'

They took off up the rough stone passageway, past the storerooms and stinking kitchens, until they reached the orange blossom and polish-scented main areas of the palace.

'OK, there's the ballroom,' muttered Ethan. 'Not far now.' He slowed to a walk and studied the polished ruby wall. 'Where's the door? I know it's here somewhere.' He ran his hands over the shiny red surface, searching for a crack or a gap to indicate where the entrance was.

'What's wrong?' asked Amber.

'I can't find the door. The Puddle people opened it from the inside when I was here last, and I nipped in when they weren't looking. I've never actually opened it.'

'What are we going to do?'

Ethan shook his head in defeat. 'We can't do anything unless we can find a way in.'

'It's not fair. Amber slumped against the wall. 'It's just not.'

The section of wall moved under her weight with a clunk. The secret door swung silently outwards, revealing the passage leading down to the fun machine.

'What did you do?' Ethan looked at Amber with

wonder.

'I don't know.'

'Well, it was brilliant.'

Amber smiled as Ethan took her hand. 'Come on,' he said. 'We've got a world to save.'

They stepped into the narrow red corridor, just as the hidden door swung shut.

'Be really quiet,' whispered Ethan. 'Up ahead is a sort of control room where a couple of scientists operate computers and stuff.'

White light spilled from the open doorway on their left. Ethan motioned for Amber to stay where she was, as he edged forwards as quietly as he could. Holding his breath, he peeked into the small room.

'Whoa! Looks like Brook and Trickle got this far, at least.'

The control room looked as though a hurricane had blown through it. The big clunky keyboard lay on the floor in a twisted heap. The TV monitors were either smashed, cracked or dangled precariously from wires. Scanning the room, he spotted both scientists amongst the wreckage.

'It's all clear,' said Ethan. 'They're out cold.'

The passageway of smooth ruby soon gave way to roughhewn rock. 'We're nearly there,' said Ethan.

'I'm scared. What if we fail?'

'We'll be all right. We've survived up until

now, haven't we?' He gave Amber's hand a gentle squeeze. Convincing his sister that everything was going to be fine wasn't easy when he thought he could hear a battle going on up ahead.

The corridor got broader the further down they went, and as they rounded the wide corner leading to the hangar door, they stopped short and backed into the shadows. Ethan's fears were, unfortunately, well founded. Up ahead were the huge door and watch towers. They were lit up brilliant white by the enormous moonstone floodlights. Icicles hung from the floodlit gantries and jutted out of the ground, like puddles frozen in mid splash.

'What's going on?' said Amber.

'Therm cannons. Look.' Ethan pointed to the watch towers.

Streams of white blasted a stack of metal packing crates, coating them in a thick layer of frost and ice.

The clear watery shape of a puddle person emerged from the shadows beside them, making Ethan jump.

'Brook Backwater is pinned down amongst those crates, and my therm pistol is out of ammo.' Seeing Ethan's look of alarm, the new arrival held up his hands.

'Sorry. I didn't introduce myself. I'm Trickle Tide, an undercover agent for the Dryads.'

Ethan looked him up and down. Tall and stick thin, Trickle Tide looked like a typical teenager, only made out of water. A dark green baseball cap with the words "Silver Ponds FC" was pulled low over an open looking face. Clear spots showed through a long greasy fringe of turquoise. Ethan's instincts told him that, in another life, he could have been really good friends with him. His instincts, however, had been badly out of tune of late. He grabbed Amber and pushed her behind him.

'How do I know it's really you? I've never met you.'

'I've been working as a cleaner in the palace, and I'm not supposed to be anywhere near the kitchens. Mrs Gurgle, the head cook, is always having a go at me because I'm forever in her way. She's a proper motor mouth, but I get good intel from her. Is that enough info for you?'

Ethan looked down at the bulbous copper therm pistol jammed in Trickle's belt.

'It's out of ammo. I told you that. Look, if you don't believe me, check it yourself.' He handed Ethan the weapon by his forefinger and thumb.

Ethan turned it over in his hands. 'OK, I believe you.'

'Uh, Mr Tide.' Amber stepped out from behind Ethan. 'What are we going to do next?'

'*We* aren't going to do anything. *I*, on the other hand, have to get across that wide floodlit gap, draw fire from Brook Backwater, so she can get into the fun machine hangar, join her somehow and destroy the fun machine. Wish me luck,' he said and ran out into the harsh glare of the flood-lights.

'Over here, you useless nimrods!' yelled Trickle, as he sprinted towards the hangar door. He zig-zagged, as icy blasts exploded around him.

'Look!' Amber pointed to the boxes. A girl elemental poked her head above the crates. 'It's Brook Backwater. I hope she makes it.'

'Let's make sure she does,' said Ethan. 'Follow me but stay close.'

Hurtling out into the danger zone, Ethan sprinted as hard as he could towards the cover of the boxes, lethal streams of hyperthermium criss-crossing in the air above his head. Glancing up, he saw Brook emerge from her hiding place and dash the short distance to the small door. She'd made it. He dived behind the crates and felt Amber slam into the back of him.

'Ethan, are you OK?' she yelled above the cannon's roar.

'Yeah, you?'

The makeshift barricade shuddered as it was struck again and again.

'What are you doing?' shouted Ethan, over the din, as Amber squeezed her head into a gap between two of the cases.

'It's Trickle,' hollered Amber. 'I thought I saw him come this way. He's been wounded.'

Trickle Tide seeped from between the two crates. He was almost entirely in liquid form, apart from his frozen right arm that scraped across the rough ground. Re-forming back into person shape, he slumped against the boxes. 'You should have gone back to the hideout with Lake.'

'We couldn't get out,' said Amber. 'The tunnel has been blocked by a rock fall.'

'There's only one way out, then,' said Trickle. 'I'll draw their fire, and you make for the small hangar door. I'll see you in a mo.'

Stepping from the cover of the boxes, Trickle shouted at the gunners in the watch towers. 'Here I am, come and get me!'

Ethan risked a glance over the parapet. 'All the focus is on Trickle. Now's our chance.' Grasping Amber firmly by the hand, he stood up and was about to run towards the door, when a voice rang out from behind him.

'Myles Ethan Myles! Stop where you are and raise your hands above your head!'

They'd been caught. A battalion of guards stepped out of the shadows. What chance did they stand against therm guns? He released his grip on Amber's hand and slowly raised his arms. Just like the throne room when he first met the emperor, he couldn't see a way out. Guards behind them, watch towers in front of them. All they had was a spotty unarmed teenager with a bad hairdo to help them.

'Oy, losers!' shouted the unarmed teenager. 'It's me you want, not them!' Jets of hyperthermium and crackling arcs of electricity blasted the jeering Trickle Tide. Ethan flinched as the Dryad spy was struck again and again. He mustn't waste Trickle's heroism with indecision. He had to act. The door to the fun machine was only a few short metres away, and he only had this one chance. He glanced at Amber. 'Run.' Without a backward glance, they sprinted out from behind the pile of cases and tore open the small door. Tumbling through it, they pulled it shut behind them.

The tropical swelter hit Ethan hard and sweat oozed from every pore. They were so close, but it was far from over. He dragged a sleeve across his face to clear his vision. 'Help me find something to jam this door with.' If they didn't at least slow the guards down, they'd fail within sight of their goal.

'What about this?' Amber held up a long broom.

'Perfect,' said Ethan and jammed it behind the door handle.

'Is that the fun machine?' Amber turned around and stared at the pulsing metal heart.

'It's…alive.' She grabbed Ethan's hand and squeezed it hard enough to hurt.

'That's what we've come to destroy.' He nodded towards the gleaming machinery.

'I can't do it.' Amber backed towards the door, pulling Ethan with her. 'I want to go home.'

'If we don't finish this, the whole world will change forever.'

'How are we even going to reach it?' Amber looked up at Ethan, dismay written all over her face. 'This place is full of people in weird diving suits. We'll never make it.'

'Psst.' Brook Backwater stepped from behind a locker, wearing one of the brown outfits but without the helmet. 'I'm going to march you across the cavern. You two pretend to be my prisoners. When we get to the fun machine, I'll cause a diversion, and both of you climb the gantry to where the rose gold crystals are. Me and Trickle can push the gantry over, leaving you to remove the crystals.' Brook looked from Ethan to Amber.

'Trickle did make it, didn't he?' Ethan shook his head, whilst Amber looked at the floor.

'My poor, poor Trickle.' Brook slid down the front of the lockers to the floor and began to weep.

'Open this door in the name of the emperor!' The door handle jiggled violently.

'I'll give you to the count of three before I blast my way in. One!'

'Get up, Brook. We've got to go.' Ethan shook the girl by the shoulders. 'Trickle wouldn't have wanted you to give up.' He grabbed her by the hand and pulled her upright.

'Two! One more second and I'm coming in.'

Brook wiped her eyes on her sleeve. 'Did he suffer?'

Amber stepped between Ethan and Brook. 'He's a hero. He saved our lives. He's the bravest person I've ever met.'

Brook smiled down at Amber and briefly hugged her. 'Hand me that helmet, would you?'

'Three!'

The door shuddered, as a volley of shots pounded it from outside. With a splintering crack, the door split open, and the guards thundered into the chamber.

'We'll take it from here.' The head guard stepped forward, arm outstretched ready to clamp Ethan's wrists with a pair of elemental shackles. With his dark blue uniform and peaked cap, the captain of the guard reminded Ethan of a New York cop. An angry white scar ran from the side of the captain's mouth, right up to his ear, giving him a permanent sneer.

'Not so fast, cowboy,' said Brook. 'I'm the head of engineering, and I have strict instructions from Doctor Freeze. If either of them is spotted in the fun machine chamber, I'm to escort them to the doctor, personally.'

'Are you sure about that?' said the captain. 'I've got orders from the emperor himself to take the prisoners to the throne room.'

'Your choice,' said Brook, hands on her hips. 'If you want to go against the wishes of Doctor Freeze, be my guest, but he won't be pleased with you.'

'Oh yes, of course,' said the captain. 'The good doctor knows best. I'll organise the troops and provide you with an armed escort. The Overlanders are extremely dangerous, after all.'

'They'll be no need. I've got it covered. Hurry up. Quick march.' Brook prodded Ethan in the back, and he stumbled forward. Sweat stung his eyes as he marched across the super-heated cavern.

'Come on!' barked Brook, as she prodded Ethan and Amber. 'You're my prisoners now, and we've got a meeting with Doctor Freeze.'

As they neared the pulsing machine, a familiar voice boomed from behind them.

'Stop them!' The temperature suddenly dropped, as a blast of frigid air swept through the huge chamber.

Ethan's heart jumped in his chest. He knew that voice. If winter could talk, it would sound like that.

'It's Doctor Freeze,' said Brook. 'Leg it!'

The guards, the guns, they were nothing in the face of deep-frozen evil.

'Follow me,' said Ethan as he took off across the chamber.

The air was alive with static electricity, as blue bolts of lightning shot from the guards' weapons. Puddle people in bulky air-conditioned suits lumbered after them. Amber skipped over a Puddle person that had made a dive for her.

'This way.' Ethan sped around to the far side of the huge beating heart.

He shoved an engineer aside, stepped onto the gantry and scrambled up to the first level. 'Take my hand!' he yelled as he reached for Amber's outstretched arm. As he pulled Amber onto the platform, a hand reached for the scaffolding and grabbed the base. Amber kicked out hard. The glass window in the brass helmet shattered.

'Ow, that hurt! It's me, Brook.' Brook Backwater removed the helmet and dropped it with a clang. Pouring herself out of the neck hole of the suit, she transformed into a whirlpool. 'Get a move on!' she yelled. 'I'll try to hold them off.'

Ethan Stepped from the top platform onto the fun machine.

With every b-boom, the metal skin of the machine expanded and contracted alarmingly. Ethan swayed, arms windmilling wildly. Dropping to his hands and knees, he crawled towards the rose gold quartz. 'Amber, are you OK?'

Amber leapt across from the top of the gantry and landed lightly. 'I'm fine, but the guards are coming. Help me push the gantry over.'

'There's no time. We've got to remove the rose gold quartz.'

'Stop them, you imbeciles! Stop them before it's too late!'

Ethan glanced at Amber and knew instantly what she was thinking. Doctor Freeze was coming. They had to work fast.

'Here it is.' Ethan pulled the screwdriver from his pocket and levered off the cover plate. Pulsing in time to the fun machine's heartbeat were the two rose gold crystals. 'The fun machine's power source. This is it.'

Amber looked up at the ornate brass clock. 'Hurry up, we're nearly out of time.'

Reaching out a hand, Amber grabbed hold of the

crystals.

'Don't!' yelled Ethan. 'It might be dangerous!'

There was a loud crack, as a blue spark jumped from the crystal. Amber screamed and flew backwards. Ethan made a grab for her as she slid over the smooth edge of the machine. B-boom. She bounced as the heart pulsed once more, her feet dangling in the air. 'Help! Don't drop me!' she shouted.

Imperial troops had now reached the fun machine. 'Freeze!' yelled the captain.

Pulling with all his might, Ethan dragged Amber back from the brink as a jet of hyperthermium shot past. 'The timer's speeding up,' said Ethan, as he scuttled across the undulating metal skin. The slow and steady beat had started to accelerate. The relaxed hiss-chuff became more urgent as the cogs and gears became a spinning blur.

'What are we going to do?' Amber stared at Ethan, eyes wide with fear.

'I've got it.' Ethan plunged a hand into his jeans pocket. Pulling out the pliers he'd found in Doctor Freeze's lab, he reached into the cavity, gripped one of the crystals and pulled.

'Five seconds until fun machine power up. Four, three...'

The public address system went quiet for a few seconds until; 'System malfunction. I repeat. System malfunction.'

'These pliers are insulated against electric shock,' said Ethan. 'We've done it.'

'Emergency override initiated,' the speakers blared. 'I repeat. Emergency override initiated.'

The counter at the base of the big brass clock clicked over.

'Two seconds until fun machine power up.'

'Overlanders!' Doctor Freeze stepped onto the upper platform of the gantry, eyes full of fury. He jumped on to the top of the fun machine and lunged for Ethan.

'One second until fun machine power up.'

Out of the corner of his eye, Ethan could see an icy blue hand reaching for him. He knew this was his last chance. He had less than one second to save all of humanity from eternal misery. Without thinking, he plunged the pliers into the crystal cavity, once again. Before his nerves could take hold, he gripped the second crystal as tightly as he could and tugged. At the exact moment Doctor Freeze grabbed Ethan's wrist, the fun machine juddered violently, cogs and pistons jamming.

'What have you done?' Doctor Freeze hauled Ethan to his feet. 'My beautiful machine! My baby! You've killed it!' he screeched. Rivets started to pop out of the metal skin, releasing whistling jets of steam. Gear wheels strained and slipped out of control, stripping metal teeth with a grinding roar. Doctor Freeze turned his attention to Amber. 'Stay right where you are,' he growled. 'I haven't finished with you, yet.'

Armed guards streamed up the gantry and piled onto the dying fun machine. 'We've got the spy in custody, sir,' said the captain. 'What shall we do with the Overlanders?'

'Shackle them. Take them to my lab. But whatever you do, don't take your eyes off them for a second.'

The loudspeakers crackled to life. 'Warning, cooling system malfunction. Evacuate fun machine cavern.'

A siren began to wail. It built in volume and pitch, until it filled the huge, steamy space.

'System meltdown imminent. Evacuate the area, immediately.' The automated voice competed hard with the siren.

'Right,' said the captain. 'Let's go.' He snapped a pair of ice handcuffs on Ethan's and Amber's wrists and hauled them to the gantry. 'You've got no idea how much trouble you're in.' He shoved them onto the top platform.

CHAPTER 16

The New Beginning

The fun machine workers gushed out of their suits and headed for the exit in a wave of panic.

'She's gonna blow!' yelled one, as he sped past.

Sporadic bursts of gunfire made Ethan drop to the ground. Glancing up, he could see rivets firing from the machine's skin, like bullets. Guards sprawled on the rough stone floor as the deadly projectiles zipped overhead. *Thwip.* Ethan flinched as the breeze from one buzzed past his right ear.

'On your feet, you cowards!' Doctor Freeze batted away the flying bolts as if they were nothing more than butterflies. The captain got to his feet, ducking as shrapnel whirred overhead.

'Yes, sir. Come on, you lot. You've got a job to do!' he barked.

Cold fingers gripped Ethan's upper arm, and he

was dragged unceremoniously upright.

'You and your sister have caused untold damage.' The frosty eyes of Doctor Freeze flashed a deep crimson. 'Now it's time for the pair of you to pay me back,' he growled.

'Not so fast, Freeze,' came a voice from behind him. The grip on Ethan's arm tightened, as he was whirled around to face the new arrival.

'Lake Splashdown, I presume,' said Doctor Freeze, in a tone that dripped sarcasm.

Ethan looked on powerlessly, as Amber struggled in the grip of the captain.

'We're leaving here, and we're taking the vermin with us.' The doctor drew a gleaming copper pistol and pressed the barrel to Ethan's temple. 'Do you comprehend? Do you… understand?'

Blinking hard to clear the sweat from his eyes, Ethan could make out a line of Dryads. They dropped their weapons and raised their arms.

'OK, OK. Just don't harm them, all right? We surrender.'

Ethan had never seen Lake give up. He watched in numb disbelief, as the pistol fell from his fingers.

'Come on, raise your arms like a good little prisoner,' said the doctor.

Lake raised his right arm, his bandaged left arm hanging limp by his side. A low rumble cut through the bells and sirens.

'Doctor!' said the captain in alarm. He was pointing at the fun machine, which had stopped hissing and now trembled violently. Huge cogs and pistons shook loose and crashed to the ground. The polished brass clock fell from its mounting. It rolled along the top of the juddering skin, before exploding in a shower of springs and gears.

'It's time to wish you farewell,' said the doctor. 'There's no point in trying to follow. The hangar door will seal shut on my command, locking you in, as this temple to my brilliance implodes, taking you with it.'

The speakers screamed with feedback. 'System meltdown imminent, evacuate the area immediately.'

'There's my cue.' The doctor took a step backwards towards the exit, dragging Ethan with him.

There was a small creak, barely audible above the din, and Ethan felt the doctor's grip loosen.

'It's time to...' The frost-bound voice cut short, as Doctor Freeze lurched sideways, flinging Ethan across the room. Ethan staggered for a few steps before his ankle folded with a white-hot burst of agony, and he crumpled into an undignified heap. His mind raced, trying to piece together what had just happened. One second he was being dragged back to the lab and the next... He struggled to get back to his feet, but an explosion of pain tore through his ankle, sending him sprawling. He fell back onto his shackled wrists. He wasn't going anywhere.

'Ethan, look out!' screamed Amber.

Ethan stared in impotent terror, as Doctor

Freeze raised the pistol and pointed it straight at him.

'I nearly had it. I nearly had it all.' The doctor's eyes changed from ice blue, through velvet purple, to deepest lacquered black. The sound of blizzard bearing winds and creaking ice howled through the cavern.

The sights and sounds of the fun machine chamber had now been distilled down to just one thing. Nothing else mattered to Ethan, as he stared down the barrel of certain death.

Time slowed to a crawl as the doctor pulled back the hammer and squeezed the trigger. That's when reality rushed back in and everything happened at once. Lake Splashdown ran headlong into Doctor Freeze, snapping off the hand holding the pistol. Amber stamped down hard on the captain's foot and kicked him in the shin, sending him reeling. Doctor Freeze's pistol fired a shot of hyperthermium directly at the fun machine, hitting the rose gold quartz compartment.

Then everything stopped. The fun machine ceased its trembling and now sat dark and silent. The sirens and alarms gradually wound down, and an unnatural quiet shrouded the vast space.

Looking around in confusion, Ethan could see the guards and Dryads just standing in absolute silence. The only movement in the whole cavern was the occasional rod or bolt clattering from the dead machine.

'Amber, are you OK?' As he tried to stand, a jagged

spear of pain flared in his ankle, and he flopped back to the ground.

'Yeah, I'm fine. You?' Amber leaned over him. 'Everyone's just sort of stopped,' she said. 'It's as if somebody's thrown a switch.'

'Get the keys out of my jeans.' Ethan gestured to his front pocket.

Pulling her knees up to her chest, Amber manoeuvred her shackled arms from around her back and slid her cuffed wrists down the back of her legs and over her feet. With her hands now in front of her, she rummaged in Ethan's pocket.

'Vermin.' Doctor Freeze turned his head to face them.

'Hurry up!' said Ethan in alarm, as the doctor creaked back to life.

'You need to be punished for what you've done.' The doctor's voice didn't sound quite as crisp as it usually did, and as he took a step, his left foot crumbled as if it were a pile of crushed ice.

The key clicked in the frozen white lock of Ethan's cuffs, and he rolled sideways, just as Doctor Freeze crashed to the floor. Amber hopped to safety and slung the ice shackles to one side. 'Ethan, get up!' she shouted.

'I can't.' The doctor grabbed his bad ankle, making him scream in agony. A pool of water was forming under Doctor Freeze and Amber slammed a boot into the back of his head. The doctor whipped around, snarling and gurgling.

'Wait until I get hold of you, girl.'

'He's melting!' shouted Amber and grabbed a twisted piston rod from the floor. She swung it as hard as she could, and it hit the side of the doctor's head with a jarring crunch. Shards of ice and droplets of water hung in the air, a rainbow arching over the stricken body.

Water gushed from the misshapen mouth of the doctor. He looked up at Amber, a grotesque parody of a grin spreading across the rapidly melting face.

Amber swung one last time. A wet splatch was followed by a crack.

The grin remained, as the doctor's head slowly canted to the left and slid off his shoulders. Out of the rapidly spreading puddle, a crimson eye flashed, before dissolving away to nothing but water.

Handing Ethan the piston rod to use as a makeshift crutch, Amber helped him to his feet. 'I think it's over,' she said.

'What's over?'

'Lake, is that you?' Ethan winced, as he hopped around to face Lake Splashdown.

'Is what me?'

Ethan rolled his eyes. 'Don't start that again.'

The Dryads, guards and workers gradually came back to life. Confused faces stared around at the destruction.

'What happened?' asked the captain. 'Why am I here?'

Ethan turned to face Amber. 'This is just like the after effect of a strong blast of fun essence.'

'I don't get it,' said Amber. 'It can't be. We destroyed the fun machine.'

Ethan scanned the chamber, and he could see weapons being set aside. The doctor's spell had finally been broken. Puddle people stared around as if seeing the cavern and the machine for the first time.

Blinking in disbelief, Ethan watched as the opposing forces greeted each other as old friends. Amiable chatter and gentle laughter filled the space left by the silent cogs and pistons. Ethan grabbed Lake by the arm and dragged him away from a conversation he was having with the captain. 'What's going on?'

Lake looked at Ethan and smiled. 'I've no idea. Have you met Captain Drain of the Imperial Guard? We served together, back in the day.'

Before Ethan could answer, a familiar voice rang out.

'Lake Splashdown!' The crowds parted as Storm Floodwater limped through the door. Storm leaned on the therm cannon that was still frozen to his arm. Dragging himself forward, cannon thumping the ground with a dull clomp, Storm hobbled towards Lake.

CHAPTER 17

The Shrinking Puddle

Silence fell as the two adversaries faced one another.

'Lake,' said Storm. A fit of uncontrollable coughing ripped through his body, doubling him over. Once the racking spasms ceased, he looked up, face etched with sorrow. 'How can I ever apologise?'

Lake stepped forward and laid a hand on Storm's shoulder. 'There's no need,' he said. 'I think we all know who the real villain is here.' He looked around as if searching for someone. 'Where's Doctor Freeze?'

'He melted,' said Amber.

Lake's features creased into a frown. 'How? When?'

'When the fun machine seized up, all of you just stopped, as if you'd been switched off.' Amber shrugged.

'Yeah,' said Ethan. 'All except the doctor, who grabbed hold of me, but Amber pounded him, and he just sort of...' He tailed off and gestured towards a puddle laying near the base of the fun machine.

'I think it's time we went to see the emperor,' said Lake.

The only sound in the packed throne room was the swish and tinkle of the emperor's ruby cloak, as he paced to and fro. His face was a picture of concentration, as he thumbed through the sheaf of notes. Stopping suddenly, he looked up from the paperwork. 'He called me a gullible fool. It's here on page twenty-five.'

Ethan watched as the emperor's expression went from disbelief, through shock, wide-eyed amazement, anger and finally incredulity. He rested the pile of notes gently on the arm of the ruby throne and turned to face the waiting crowd. After what felt to Ethan like an eternity, he spoke in a slow measured tone.

'First of all, I offer my sincere apologies to the Dryads, all of whom I give an unconditional pardon.' Cheers echoed around the high domed room. The emperor lifted a hand and the whoops and halloos faded away. 'Secondly...' the emperor's eyes went wide when a cracked and rasping voice drifted from the rear of the room.

'Emperor Monsoon!' Eldermaster Rain shuffled towards the dais and climbed the steps. Standing face to face with the emperor, he threw his arms wide. 'I've missed you, brother.' Emperor Monsoon and the eldermaster embraced, rubies and emeralds mingling as their cloaks swished together.

'They're brothers?' Ethan stared from the throne to Lake.

'Eldermaster Rain was Monsoon's head of technology, until Freeze stole his lab notes and falsified the results,' said Lake. 'He made it look as if the eldermaster was planning to overthrow the emperor. Word got around regarding the whole affair, which pushed Puddlemere to the brink of civil war. It nearly tore our civilisation apart.' Lake shook his head. 'They haven't spoken to each other since Black Funday.'

The emperor clapped twice. 'Silence, everyone. My brother wishes to speak.'

Leaning on his emerald staff, Eldermaster Rain lifted his head. 'As you are all aware, I was accused of treason.' Murmurs rumbled through the assembly. 'These notes belonging to Doctor Freeze, not only prove my innocence but condemn the doctor as the guilty party.' He held the sheaf of paper above his head, and a small yellow note slid out, fluttering gently to the floor.

The emperor scooped it up and scanned the memo. 'Sorry to interrupt you, but I think this could be important.' He handed the note to the eldermaster.

Holding up a hand to quiet the murmuring crowd, the eldermaster cleared his throat. 'This disturbing information confirms that Doctor Freeze intended to destroy our government and take control of Puddlemere. I shall read it to you all. *The side effects of fun essence.*' His eyes flicked across the memorandum. '*Initial tests revealed short-term memory loss, lethargy and insomnia.*'

Ethan watched the eldermaster's finger trace the writing across the paper.

'*Further tests prove conclusively that high doses cause negative personality defects, including distrust and disharmony between friends and family. Over a prolonged period, it is likely to result in the breakdown of the social fabric of our society, thus allowing me to assert control.*' He looked up. 'There's a handwritten notation at the bottom. *Aim to increase the dose to maximum strength asap.* I think we can all agree that we've been experiencing negative and confusing emotions.'

Mumbled agreements rippled through the group.

'For your returned natural fun essence, you have Myles Ethan Myles and Amber to thank.'

All eyes turned to Ethan and his sister. A slow and steady chant of 'Speech, speech, speech,' rose in volume, until both kids were ushered to the side of the throne.

Emperor Monsoon knelt before them. 'For the wrongs I have done you, I do not expect forgiveness. I wish I could take back my words and deeds. You have restored our natural fun essence and saved your own race. As a token of my undying gratitude, I will give you anything within my power. Anything at all, just name it.'

Diamonds, rubies and riches beyond measure filled Ethan's mind, but before he could utter a word, his thoughts turned to home. Mum's lung disease. She was filling up with fluid, which meant she would eventually drown on dry land. Drown. Drown? He could breathe underwater. It was impossible for him to drown, and that was all thanks to... 'Puddle draught!' He blurted the words out, making the emperor jump. 'Puddle draught,' he repeated. 'If it's all right, I'd like a gallon of puddle draught.'

Amber stared at him in disbelief. 'With all the gems in this place, you go and pick a drink?'

He took her by the shoulders. 'That allows you to breathe under water. Don't you get it?'

'Get what?' She shook her head.

'It's for Mum. Her lung disease means she'll drown in her own fluids, but if she drinks puddle draught...'

She cut him off. 'You're a genius.' She hugged him so tightly, he thought she'd crush him.

'Yes please,' she said, as she turned back to face the emperor. 'I'd like the same, please.'

The emperor rose slowly to his feet. 'Very well. If that's your wish.' He paused before snapping his fingers. 'I nearly forgot.' He withdrew both of the rose gold quartz crystals from the folds of his cloak. 'These are for you.' Engraved on each crystal were the words *For bravery above and beyond the call of duty and services to Puddlemere during the Great Fun War.* Tied to each crystal with a pale blue ribbon was a polished brass cross with the words *Monsoon medal for bravery* etched across its surface.

Ethan gulped back the lump that had formed in his throat. 'I, I don't know what to say,' he stuttered.

As if to save him from an embarrassing speech, thunderous applause erupted from the crowd.

'I'd just like to say that Amber and I...' Ethan stopped mid-sentence. 'The puddle! What about the puddle?'

A puzzled expression played on the emperor's face. 'What puddle?'

'The puddle in the park. You told me that once it had dried out, we'd be stuck here forever.'

'By all that's wet and wonderful, I'd forgotten all about that,' said the emperor in alarm.

'Mum and Dad are going to have a kitten fit,' said Ethan. 'We've been gone for days. We'll be beyond grounded.'

'Don't worry,' said the emperor.

'What?' said Amber. 'Don't tell me you're going to show up on the doorstep and explain everything to them. They'll blow a brain gasket.'

'Time runs differently here in Puddlemere,' said the emperor. 'Two days here is roughly the same as two hours in Overland. Think about it. The puddle would have been long gone if a full two days had passed, and I have it on good authority that it's still there.' He got to his feet and straightened his cloak.

'Colonel Splashdown!' he barked.

Lake looked quizzically at the emperor.

'Don't look so surprised, man. I've just reinstated you. Organise transport back to Silver Ponds for our guests.'

Lake Splashdown snapped to attention and flicked off a salute. 'Right away, Your Highness.'

'Captain Drain, get a ladder to the King Tower stalagmite, pronto!'

The captain saluted, before rushing from the room.

'Myles Ethan Myles, Amber. Before you go, I'd just like to assure you that the fun essence that was stolen from your world will be returned. My brother and I will work together to ensure this happens. Now hurry, before the puddle dries out.'

The stalagmite looked much bigger than Ethan remembered. It soared upwards, like the pictures he'd seen of the New York skyscrapers. A shaft of bright sunlight speared from a tiny patch of pale blue, high above. It lit the top of the rock tower, like a snow-capped mountain. Resting against the side of the stone monolith was the biggest ladder Ethan had ever seen. Wooden rungs stretched up into the sky, like a vertical railway line. Staring up at them made him feel dizzy.

'That's a seriously long way up,' said Amber, breathlessly.

'No kidding.' Ethan limped forwards and gripped the wooden rails. 'I hope my ankle holds up.'

'You'll be fine,' said Lake. 'Take it one step at a time, and whatever you do, don't look down.' He turned himself into a high-powered jet of water and shot up the rock face. 'See you at the top,' he shouted down and disappeared from view.

'You go first,' said Amber. 'I'll be right behind you.'

Testing his bad ankle, Ethan put his weight fully onto the bottom rung. The searing pain had now mellowed to a dull throb, pulsing in time with his heartbeat. As long as he was careful, he might just be able to make it. He placed one foot above the other and had settled into a steady rhythm, when his throbbing ankle flared. Twisting sideways, his leg collapsed from under him, flinging him into space. He reached out and grasped the wooden rail. Gripping with all his might, he hauled himself back onto the ladder, gasping with the pain and effort. The world slid to the right.

'We're going to fall!' Amber screamed. The whole structure slipped away from the rock face at an alarming rate. Ethan held on and braced himself for impact, when suddenly everything stopped. They were no longer falling. Instead, they were being pulled upright.

'You don't seriously think I'd let you fall, do you?' Lake's voice drifted from high above. 'Now, get a move on. The puddle is getting dangerously small.'

Ethan took a deep breath. 'I can do this,' he said under his breath. Pulling on the rungs, he hopped to the next step. It wasn't going to be easy, but he had to keep the weight off his bad foot.

'Ethan, look at the puddle,' said Amber.

He stared upwards to where the sun filtered down into Puddlemere and instead of the bright shaft of light, there was now an extra patch of darkness.

'We're too late.' He hung his head. 'The puddle's gone. We're stuck here forever. Only a hundred metres to go, as well. We nearly made it.'

'We still can,' said Amber, excitedly. 'Look!'

Ethan lifted his head to see the sun break out from behind a cloud. The patch of sky high above them lit up a brilliant shade of late summer blue. A searchlight beam speared the gloom, spurring Ethan into action. He dragged himself up to where Lake was waiting.

'You two took your time, didn't you?' Reaching out a hand, Lake pulled Ethan onto the top of the stalagmite. 'We haven't got much time. The portal is about to close, so I need both of you to stand just there.' He pointed to the small pool that Ethan had fallen into when he first entered Puddlemere. 'Hold on tight and get ready for lift off.' Lake turned himself into a column of water and dropped to the floor.

The pool that Ethan and Amber were standing

in started to bubble and froth, as a fountain of solid water lifted them towards the opening high above.

Cut grass, hot tarmac, and the distant aroma of someone's backyard barbecue filled Ethan with the smell of home. He squinted in the brightness and stumbled forwards onto the grass, where he flopped down. Shielding his eyes with his hand, he could see Amber standing next to Lake Splashdown. The sun shone through Lake, making him almost invisible in the white summer light.

'Myles Ethan Myles, Amber. Thank you for everything. I can't stick around, so goodbye. You never know, we may meet again.'

Before either of them could speak, Lake dropped through the puddle with barely a ripple.

'Mum, Dad, we're home,' Ethan called out as he opened the front door. The cool autumnal weather had turned, bringing summer back with a flourish. Following the delicious odour of grilling sausages and burgers, Ethan and Amber made their way through the house into the back garden. Blue smoke drifted on charcoal scented air.

'Oh hello, you two.'

Dad sounded distracted. He paced up and down in front of the barbecue with his mobile phone clamped to his ear.

'What's wrong?' Ethan knew it was something

bad. It couldn't be the car; Dad wouldn't look so worried. 'Where's Mum?'

Dad stopped pacing. 'She's resting.'

Resting. That was Dad-code for very ill. He knew how to read the signs. The pacing, the phone, and the pale drawn expression.

'Grab yourself a burger from the barbie. They should be ready by now.' Dad waved a hand distractedly over the sizzling grill.

'Yeah,' said Ethan. 'In a bit. I just need to use the loo, first.' He nodded briefly to Amber. He knew she'd sussed what he was about to do. Dad was on the phone to the hospital; Ethan just knew it. Mum was going back in, so he had to give her the puddle draught before the ambulance arrived. Once she was in the hands of the paramedics, he'd never be able to give it to her. He'd left the puddle draught hidden behind the bag of cat grit by the front door. How could he possibly explain a decanter carved from a solid lump of quartz, suddenly appearing out of nowhere? He'd found it in the park and was going to feed its unknown, possibly toxic contents to Mum? Yeah, right. He grabbed a coffee cup from the kitchen on his way to the front door. Dad was still on the phone, so he had enough time.

❖ ❖ ❖

'Mum?' A gurgling wheeze sounded from the bedroom. It was more pronounced. Louder than when he'd last heard it. No wonder Dad had called the hospital. He eased the door open a crack, his heart thundering in his chest. His hands felt clammy in the cool, disinfected air. A shaft of sunlight lasered through the gap in the curtains. He stopped, barely daring to breathe. Would this actually work? What if it made things worse? He stared at his mum's face. It didn't look real. It was waxy and pale. The bedclothes moved rhythmically up and down in time with her thin breaths, but only just. The two voices in his head tried to shout each other down. *Do it. Don't do it. She'll die if you do it. She'll die if you don't.* The worrying indecision was making him feel physically sick. He had to act. One way or another, he just had to do something.

'Mum, I've brought you something to drink.' There was no going back now.

'Ethan, is that you?'

The voice was weak and so unlike Mum as to be almost unrecognisable. 'Yeah, it's me. I've brought you something.' He sat down on the edge of the bed and watched as Mum dragged herself painfully into a sitting position.

'Oh, that's kind of you.'

She took the mug and sniffed the contents.

'What's this? We haven't got any mint drink.'

'Just something I got down the corner shop,' he lied. 'It will make you feel better.' He hoped, he really hoped.

She smiled. The smile seemed sort of hollow, somehow, with a deep sadness behind it. Ethan took a breath and held it. Mum raised the cup to her pallid lips. This was it. It was either going to work or it wasn't. If he kept his face neutral, then Mum wouldn't suspect anything.

He felt himself staring, so he looked away. She took a sip, looked up with a puzzled expression, then drained the contents in one.

'What is this stuff?'

She straightened up and stared into the empty cup. 'Have you got any more?'

'Dad. Mum wants burger, sausage and coleslaw.' Ethan grabbed the tongs from the garden table and started piling a plate with food. 'And ketchup. I'd better grab the bottle from the kitchen cupboard.'

Amber tilted her head. He knew that expression. It was a question, and he knew the answer. He nodded, smiling broadly.

For details of further releases by Tommy Ellis, log onto his Facebook Page @tommyellisauthor

Printed in Great Britain
by Amazon

18510246R00113